They're a big hit . . . with the enemy.

The baseball bat came within inches of Jo's skull as the bikers raced by again. They screeched to a halt like before, but this time they were much closer. The Spy Girls had seconds to act.

"That's *it!*" Jo screamed. "That came very close to the hair!"

"What are you going to do?" Theresa asked desperately, watching in obvious horror as Jo stood up, grabbed a hunk of discarded wood, and marched defiantly to the middle of the alley.

"Hey!" Jo called. "You! Yeah, you, the ugly one with the bat!" Jo brandished her own rickety club. "If you're so tough, why don't you come fight like a man!"

"Jo! He'll kill you!" Theresa pleaded.

But it was too late. Jo planted her feet and took her best Mark McGwire batting stance—but instead of a pitcher, she faced another hitter. One with a real bat.

The biker gunned the engine and raced forward, gaining m   . The rider held the ba   could survive it. This wa   r.

Jo wanted to

It happened: impact.

Don't miss any books in this thrilling new series:

#1 License to Thrill
#2 Live and Let Spy
#3 Nobody Does It Better
#4 Spy Girls Are Forever
#5 Dial "V" for Vengeance
#6 If Looks Could Kill

Available from ARCHWAY Paperbacks

If Looks
Could Kill

by
Elizabeth Cage

AN ARCHWAY PAPERBACK
Published by POCKET BOOKS
New York London Toronto Sydney Tokyo Singapore

AN ARCHWAY PAPERBACK *Original*

An Archway Paperback published by
POCKET BOOKS, a division of Simon & Schuster Inc.
1230 Avenue of the Americas, New York, NY 10020

Spy Girls™ is a trademark of 17th Street Productions,
a division of Daniel Weiss Associates, Inc.

Produced by 17th Street Productions,
a division of Daniel Weiss Associates, Inc.
33 West 17th Street, New York, NY 10011

ISBN: 0-671-03566-5

First Archway Paperback printing July 1999

10 9 8 7 6 5 4 3 2 1

AN ARCHWAY PAPERBACK and colophon are
registered trademarks of Simon & Schuster Inc.

Printed in the U.S.A.

IL 7+

To The Dude:
The new adventure is about to begin.

If Looks
Could Kill

"Somewhere there's a convertible missing its fuzzy dice," Caylin Pike remarked as she stroked the sleeve of an obnoxious purple mohair sweater.

"Some people pay a lot of money to look like fuzzy dice," Jo Carreras replied, glancing at the price tag on the garment. "But it's not *quite* me."

"Are you kidding?" Caylin said with a laugh. "It looks like someone skinned Barney."

Jo rolled her eyes. "I forgot who I was browsing with. If it can't be sweated in, it's not fit to be worn, right, Cay?"

She and Caylin continued their mondo browse fest, chatting and maneuvering between close-knit racks of endless fashion.

It's nice to have some downtime, Jo thought. Seems like we spend every waking moment trying to save the free world, but we hardly ever have a spare minute to enjoy our American-born right to shop till we drop.

But the time was *now*.

She and Cay were on the fifth floor of Bogart's, one of the biggest and most exclusive department stores in New York City. Although few and way too far between, shopping sprees were one of the many perks of being a Spy Girl. From the moment they had walked through the front door, they had been assaulted by infinite temptations and combinations: dresses, blouses, suits, sweaters. Cotton, polyester, wool, knit blends. Ah, but then they also had to accessorize: earrings, bags, shoes, fragrances, scarves. The sheer amount of merchandise was almost too much for a Spy Girl to comprehend.

Almost.

Jo was all over everything. Playing dress up was her second-favorite contact sport, after saving the world. Which she had actually done a few times. As a Spy Girl she had defused bombs, been shot at from snowmobiles, and fallen out of airplanes. Not to mention the many times she had used her stunning good looks to turn the heads of several charming enemies of the state.

Could she help it that bad guys seemed drawn to her flowing dark hair? Her black eyes and Latina complexion? Her flawless fashion sense? The only problem was her tendency to fall for the wrong men at the wrong times.

Oh, well, she thought. No one said world peace was easy.

Caylin Pike wasn't so flighty, Jo knew. Her idea of a good time was slipping her long blond hair into a ponytail, slapping on the gloves, and having a long session of kick boxing. How savage. Her fashion desires ran more toward cross trainers and running tights. But for this little excursion she had settled for jeans and a baseball jersey.

Sometimes Jo just didn't understand that girl. But baseball players *were* kind of cute. . . .

Caylin and Jo made up two-thirds of the team known as the Spy Girls. They had been recruited from their various real lives as teenagers and trained in the art of espionage.

If you asked Jo, they had become quite good, thank you very much.

During one late-night movie fest with the other girls, Jo had offered her theory why they had taken to spying so easily: Teenagers are already superspies. They are world-class information gatherers (gossip and secrets), superb infiltrators (sneaking into the movies and hot new nightclubs), and expert evaders (ditching school and ducking teachers). Just add in some language and weapons training and presto! Jane Bond is born.

Jo sighed and gazed helplessly at the endless racks all around her. "I'll need *at least* three days to do this store right."

"No dice," Caylin replied. "Uncle Sam gave us the afternoon, not the month."

"An afternoon in New York City is the equivalent of three seconds. You can't accomplish anything!"

"My heart pumps Prada for you, Jo," came a voice from behind them.

Jo and Caylin turned and saw a girl their own age. She had brown hair, girl-next-door good looks, and an armful of beautiful blouses. Like, *twenty* of them!

"Doing a little shopping, T.?" Caylin joked.

"Ha ha," Theresa Hearth replied. "These shirts have my mother's label inside."

"So?" Jo asked. "Your mother does some hot stuff. It deserves to be in Bogart's." Theresa's mother had designed a hot new line of clothing called Girl Talk. She'd been featured on everything from VH-1 to E! to *Access Hollywood*. *Very* cool.

But Jo knew that Theresa wasn't the type to get sucked into that fabulous world of haute couture and even more haute attitude. She'd rather have her nose pressed up against a computer monitor, hacking into the CIA or something—and she had several times, actually.

"That's the problem," Theresa said, dumping the pile on a display table full of gloves. "These are *supposed* to be my mother's. But they aren't."

"What do you mean? There's the Girl Talk label right under your nose," Jo pointed out.

Theresa shook her head. "They're fake. See the capital *G* and *T*?"

"So?" Caylin asked.

"My mom's label never has any capital letters," Theresa explained. "When I was little, I refused to ever use capital letters when I was learning the alphabet. So as a sort of inside joke, my mother made the labels that way. No one else knows about it."

"Stupid question," Jo said, folding her arms over her chic leather jacket. "Why wouldn't you use capital letters when you were little?"

"Because they beat up on the lowercase letters," Theresa replied, as if it were the most obvious reason in the world.

Jo rolled her eyes. "Whatever."

"What?" Theresa exclaimed. "It makes perfect sense to me!"

"Why don't you just use all capital letters?" Caylin suggested. "Then no lowercase letters will get hurt."

It was Theresa's turn to roll her eyes. "Yeah, right. Why don't you just call them 'lower-class' letters? No one would ever use them!"

"Girls—," Jo began.

"Well, if you had your way, no one would ever use capital letters. It's the same thing!" Caylin argued.

"It is not!"

"Girls—"

"It is, too!" Caylin exclaimed. "That's why they *have* upper- and lowercase letters. So you use them both. Then no one gets hurt."

Theresa was all attitude. "That is so stupid. I never—"

"*Girls!*"

Caylin and Theresa glared at Jo. "*What?*"

"Were those letters capital enough for you?" Jo asked, hands on hips. "I think it's time to go."

"I thought we were shopping," Caylin said.

Jo sighed, planted a hand on each of their shoulders, and moved them along. "You've shopped enough."

Caylin Pike loved the city.

It's like a perpetual motion machine, she thought. No one ever stops. Not for a second. A subtle smile crossed her face. Just like me.

Outside Bogart's, Fifth Avenue was truly hopping. Tourists lined up everywhere for Rockefeller Center, St. Patrick's Cathedral, and an endless selection of the most deliciously shoppable boutiques this side of Beverly Hills.

Caylin threw her arm out to flag a cab.

"We'll never get a cab at this time of day," Jo said, struggling with two large shopping bags.

"Oh, ye of little or no faith," Caylin replied. "I've got a system."

"A system? For flagging cabs?" Jo commented. "I swear, between T.'s capital letters and your 'system,' you make Dilbert look like a well-adjusted human being."

Before she could say any more, a bright yellow minivan pulled up to the curb right in front of Caylin. She turned to Jo and grinned. "You were saying?"

Jo's mouth dropped open in surprise, but she recovered quickly. "I stand by my previous insult."

"I forgive you," Caylin replied, feeling triumphant.

The three Spy Girls piled in with their various bags, stuffing themselves into the backseat of the van like sardines. Finally Theresa managed to shut the door.

"Where to, baby cakeses?" growled the heavyset driver, who came complete with a tweed hat and chewed-up cigar.

Caylin blinked, unable to believe her ears. "Did I just hear . . . did you hear . . . did he just call us 'baby cakeses'?"

"Yes, he did," Theresa replied.

"*Baby cakeses?*" Caylin repeated.

"Relax, Cay, this is New York," Jo said. "He meant it as a compliment. Right, honey buns?"

The driver winked and puffed his cigar. "Whatever you say, cupcake."

"Yeah, right, scuzzlebutt," Caylin grumbled, folding her arms and sinking into her seat.

"Where are we going?" Theresa asked.

"We have some time," Jo replied. "Another store?"

Theresa suddenly grinned. "I have an idea. Tower Records! Get it?"

"Oh, har-dee-har-har," Caylin muttered.

The organization that had recruited them, trained them, and assigned them to various missions was known only as The Tower. Caylin and the Spy Girls didn't know much about the organization at all. Their contact was called Uncle Sam, and they *never* saw his face. He was usually just a distorted image on a TV screen. That was the extent of their knowledge. They were on a need-to-know basis, and apparently their need to know was considered needless.

"Sure, Tower Records. Why not?" Caylin replied, looking out the window at the swiftly moving traffic.

"Abso-friggin'-lutely, apples of my eye," the driver said, setting the meter and roaring into traffic with a squeal of the tires. Horns blared angrily from behind them, and the girls scrambled for their seat belts.

Suddenly a voice filled the cab—what would normally be some New York celebrity reminding passengers to buckle up for safety. This voice was indeed familiar, but it didn't belong to a celebrity.

"Hello, Spy Girls, this is your Uncle Sam

reminding you to buckle up and enjoy the ride. But I'm afraid Tower Records is no longer on the agenda."

"Uncle Sam!" Jo piped up, looking around for the speakers. "Are you cleverly tucked in the glove compartment again?"

"Not even close, Jo," Sam replied.

"Are you at least in the same time zone?" Caylin asked, smiling at her friends. They all knew they weren't getting any 411 out of Sammy-poo.

"I'm afraid I can't divulge that information," Sam said smoothly.

"Shocker," Caylin quipped.

"But I bet you're going to divulge the socks off our next mission, right?" Theresa surmised.

Sam chuckled. "Sometimes you girls are just too smart for me."

"What is it this time, Sam?" Jo asked, leaning forward in her seat. "London? Paris? Gstaad?"

"How about Kinh-Sanh?"

Caylin's heart dropped. The girls stared at each other. "Kinh-Sanh?" Theresa replied uneasily.

Kinh-Sanh was an island nation halfway around the world, not far from the Chinese coast. It wasn't exactly known for its glamour.

"Isn't that a long way to go for a trio of American girls with no knowledge of Asian languages?" Jo asked.

"Relax, Spy Girls," Sam said, laughter in his

tone. "It's beautiful this time of year. And it's home to the perfect mission for you. Kinh-Sanh has become a prime tourist spot—especially for young European and American college students who backpack across Asia. It's quite the hotbed for rich young westerners looking for adventure."

"Yeah, we all read *The Beach*, Sammy," Jo replied.

"Of course. Apparently it seems that a good number of these rich young westerners are going to Kinh-Sanh but not coming home. They've joined with a man known as 'Luscious' Lucien West."

"'Luscious'?" Caylin asked, raising one perfectly shaped blond eyebrow. "You're joking."

Sam sighed. "You girls know I don't have a sense of humor."

"It's what we like best about you," Jo replied. "Continue, please."

"Right away, young lady," Sam said dryly. "It seems this West runs a religious sect from a compound a few miles outside the capital city. And it's plush. Very opulent, very private, and very hush-hush."

"My kind of joint," Jo remarked.

"Backpackers get word of this place from an underground network running throughout Southeast Asia, and they flock to Lucien West— along with the account numbers of their trust funds," Sam said.

"Sounds like a cult," Caylin said. She leaned

back into the seat as the taxicab left Manhattan for JFK Airport.

"Yes, it does," Sam agreed.

"So what does the Tower want with a self-professed holy man?" Theresa asked, squinting slightly.

The once surly driver slid a dossier through the opening in the Plexiglas partition. "Here you are, ladies," he said, harsh New York accent and chewed-up cigar now gone.

They flipped it open and read while Sam spoke. Several satellite photos—super–zoom lens close—were clipped to the dossier. "The problem is that Lucien West's physical profile matches that of an international con man known only by the name of Carruthers. He's a chameleon."

"So we see," Theresa said, passing several photos of men with blond hair, black hair, mustaches, beards, and a dozen kinds of glasses. "This is all the same guy?"

"Yes. For the past ten years Carruthers has been linked with various schemes in Europe and the United States. Mostly things like counterfeiting, con games, and gambling. But he's never been caught."

"Again I ask why the Tower cares about a con man fleecing some rich Euro-dweebs who don't know any better?" Jo inquired, studying a photo of Carruthers wearing, of all things, a turban.

"Carruthers came to the attention of The Tower when he was linked to a group of terrorists trying to smuggle nuclear weapons out of Russia," Sam answered gravely.

"Whoa," Caylin replied. "Nukes?"

"Yes, Caylin. Nukes," Sam said. "The plot failed, but again he was not caught. It's been three years since Carruthers has surfaced, and there's a good chance that this 'Luscious' Lucien West is his latest guise. And as peace loving and charismatic as Lucien is purported to be, he could be hiding something sinister . . . and deadly."

"But what if this Lucien guy is the real deal?" Jo asked, glancing warily at her friends.

"That's precisely what you're going to find out," Sammy replied.

Nothing like walking in blind, Caylin thought. "Great," she said. "But what if he's not?"

"That, Spy Girls," Sam said ominously, "is precisely for you to take care of."

This is *wild*," Theresa remarked as the Spy Girls slowly moved through the crowded streets of Kinh-Sanh's capital city. The culture shock was instantaneous—no matter how many countries they were sent to, Theresa never got over the first few minutes. "It's so alive!"

After the eternal flight across the Pacific, a taxi had sounded like torture. So to take them to their Kinh-Sanh digs, the Spy Girls hired a rickshaw—sort of a human-drawn cart. The driver just chugged along, seeming unfazed by the load he was carrying—three Spy Girls plus luggage. His only reaction when they flagged him was to glare at their pile of bags, roll his eyes, and say something unintelligible.

The capital was a beautiful city. Modern skyscrapers mingled with more traditional architecture, blending the Old World with the New. According to the Spy Girls' briefing, the prime minister of Kinh-Sanh had set forth a bold plan to modernize his country so that it might grow into a major trading power with the United States. Kinh-Sanh was known for its clothing industry—as well as its burgeoning computer industry. The tiny nation wasn't far from becoming a young Singapore. The streets were clean and safe, the citizens were educated, and the country was definitely on the upswing.

No wonder all the Western kids traveling across Asia stopped off here, Theresa thought. *This place is so cool.*

The rickshaw driver rolled them through the market district, a zoo of merchants, tourists, and native shoppers haggling over fish, bread, and cheesy souvenirs. Theresa soaked it all up, knowing that they were about to undertake a mission in the most exotic locale yet.

Finally the streets thinned out, and the driver stopped in front of a squat apartment building.

"I guess this is it," Jo said. She peeled off some Kinh-Sanh currency—known as the *yingling*—and passed it to the driver. She also slipped him a U.S. ten-dollar bill with it. "Forgive the obnoxious American, buddy, but you deserve it after hauling *our* luggage."

The man smiled and jogged off.

"Looks like we lug our own bags," Theresa said, glumly staring at all her stuff, then at the building. "To the *third* floor."

Caylin slung her backpack over one shoulder.

"You girls really need to learn how to pack light."

"Show me some computer hardware that weighs less than a hundred pounds and I'll pack it," Theresa grumbled, hefting her twin duffels.

"No one said you had to bring HAL 9000," Jo muttered. "You *always* bring HAL 9000. And his family, too."

"You glam queens have no appreciation of the fine art of hacking," Theresa replied as they entered the building and began the long climb to the third floor. "This is precision equipment. Unlike your crate o' Esteé Lauder, Jo."

"A small price to pay for world peace," Jo replied with a sigh.

Several minutes of bickering later, the girls found their apartment. Theresa produced the key that had been included in their mission pouch and opened the door.

All three of them gasped.

Unbelievable, Theresa marveled silently, mouth gaping.

"Am I wrong, or is this pad the paddiest pad yet?" Jo asked breathlessly.

"Pretty paddy," Caylin agreed.

The whole place was decorated in traditional Kinh-Sanh, complete with what appeared to be antique vases, rugs, screens, and figurines. Huge windows illuminated the twelve-foot walls with streaks of late-afternoon sunlight, bathing the apartment in an exotic orange. There was no furniture per se. There were, however, dozens of huge throw pillows and mats. In fact, the sunken center of the living room was a sea of velvet and chenille.

"I feel like a stupid American," Theresa mumbled, shaking her head. "If I had taken the time to learn anything about Kinh-Sanh culture, I'm sure I'd appreciate this a whole lot more."

"I dunno," Jo replied incredulously. "I'm appreciating it pretty well over here. And I don't even know how to ask, 'Where's the bathroom?'"

Reluctantly they dispersed to find the bedrooms, the kitchen, and for Theresa what would serve as a computer and communications room. In this area there were ports for all her equipment, along with a normal desk and chair. There were also three ten-speed mountain bikes hanging from the ceiling. Once Theresa saw the computer ports, the spell was broken for her.

"Jackpot," she whispered.

She returned to the main room to fetch her bags so she could set up shop immediately.

"Well, I'm not unpacking," Caylin said with a sigh. "I've got to jam."

Jo raised her eyebrows. "Already?"

"We just got here," Theresa added.

Caylin nodded. "I know. But if I'm going to make Lucien's compound by nightfall, I have to head out now. The map says it's ten miles."

Caylin had been elected—actually, Uncle Sam did the electing—to infiltrate Lucien West's cult, posing as yet another American backpacking across Asia with a pile of cash burning a big hole in her pocket.

"What kind of toys did Sammy give you?" Theresa asked, referring to the special-ops equipment that they were each issued at the beginning of each mission.

Caylin smiled and held up an object the size of a lipstick.

"That's *it?*" Jo asked.

"That's it," Caylin replied, zipping up her hooded fleece sweatshirt. "One miniature cell phone for emergency use only."

"What's the number?" Theresa asked.

"No number," Caylin said as she pocketed the phone. "It's one-way only. I can call you, but you can't call me. It wouldn't be too cool if you called me and this thing went off in the middle of a prayer circle or something."

"Guess not," Jo said grimly. "You be careful."

"Tell that to Luscious," Caylin replied. Theresa watched as she went into the computer room and unhooked a mountain bike from the rack. Then she shouldered her backpack, pulled the straps tight, and grabbed the bike. At the door Caylin stopped and turned.

"Later, Spy Girls."

Jo and Theresa waved, and with a deep breath Caylin left to go infiltrate the compound of Luscious Lucien West. After she was gone, Theresa turned to Jo. "I hate it when we split up."

"I know," Jo replied, shoulders slumping. "It's like we're missing a wheel."

Theresa smirked. "That would make us a tricycle, Jo."

Jo nodded. "Yeah. So?"

"Nothing—forget it." Theresa shook her head. "Do you think Cay'll be all right?"

Jo flopped down onto a pile of luxurious pillows and sighed. "She's cut off from her network. She's alone in a foreign country with no knowledge of the language or customs. She's infiltrating the home of a criminal who may or may not be up to something incredibly tacky." Jo smiled. "Of course she'll be okay."

Theresa pounded away on the keyboard like Elton John after a bad interview. Try as she might, she couldn't hack into Lucien West's files.

"I'm becoming *extremely* peeved," she warned the room. "Nobody needs this much security on their files. Madonna doesn't have this much security."

Just then Jo sashayed into the computer room. She spun around to show off her freshly unpacked ensemble of ribbed cotton tank top, black leggings, and flowing black kimono with an intricate dragon design. "What do you think of my 'first-day-in-Kinh-Sanh' selection, T.?"

Theresa tore her eyes away from the screen long enough to look Jo over. "East meets West in a head-on collision. Call the paramedics."

Jo's hands went to her hips faster than you could say *unsolicited attack.* "Well, we're a walking pile of personal problems today, aren't we?"

"It's our buddy, Luscious," Theresa said, gesturing at her machine.

Jo came closer and squinted at the screen. "Problem, O Goddess of the Technogeeks?"

Theresa finished a particularly feverish bout of typing and turned to her partner. "It's like Fort Knox, Jo. It's like this Luscious is hiding the next big entry in the burger wars or something. I can't get in anywhere! Auuugh!" She growled and tapped more keys. Tapped. Growled. Tapped. Then pounded the keyboard in frustration. "And what kind of a name is *Luscious,* anyway? What is he, a professional wrestler?"

Suddenly Theresa's computer let out an angry beep.

Theresa gulped. "Uh-oh."

Jo stiffened. "What is it?"

It beeped again.

Theresa typed wildly, alternating between her keyboard and her mouse. "Whoa," she said. "Whoa . . . *whoa!*"

Theresa lunged across the desk and yanked the cord out of her modem. Then she kicked the power cord out of the wall. She reclined in her chair and sighed. "That was way uncalled for."

"What was?" Jo asked, clueless.

Theresa shook her head in disbelief. "I haven't seen anything like that since the CIA," she said.

"Come on, girl, speak!" Jo growled in frustration. "Anything like *what?*"

"Watch this." Theresa reattached all her wires and hit the power switch. Her laptop came on, but the screen was blank. No cursor, no intro screen, no nothing.

"What does that mean?" Jo asked with a shrug.

Theresa sighed and slumped into her chair. "It means I got nuked in a big way. The security program on Lucien's network destroyed my computer. Everything's gone. It's useless."

"Wow," Jo said, stroking her jaw. "He can do that?"

"He just did." Theresa shook her head. "This is some serious stuff. Whoever set up Lucien's net is a true ace. This is government-level watchdog programming. And it took a bite out of me. I need a new computer!"

"We'll have to request one from Sammy," Jo said.

Theresa chuckled. "He'll be happy to hear about that."

"Did you find anything at all?"

Theresa snapped up the lone printout she could extract from the computer. "It looks like Lucien's corporation has extensive holdings in the city. But the only thing concrete I could find was this." She handed over the page to Jo. "It's a warehouse down on the waterfront. Supposedly he's going to use it for some future recreation facility. But right now it's empty."

"Okay," Jo replied, nodding. "So that leaves us with two questions."

Theresa ran her hands through her dark hair and blew out an exasperated breath. "Two questions?"

Jo nodded. "One, what would a second-rate religious cult leader need with world-class security on his computer files?"

"Unless he had something world-class to hide," Theresa replied. "So what's the second question?"

"The second question is even simpler."

"Yeah?"

A smile crept onto Jo's face. "Why aren't we hauling buns down to the waterfront to check out that warehouse?"

*   *   *

Caylin huffed and puffed and pedaled. Normally a ten-mile bike ride wouldn't have been that big a deal for her. But add a big backpack to the equation and the steep hills of the Kinh-Sanh countryside, and Caylin was beat.

The road was paved, but narrow and winding. No cars passed her. In fact, once she left the city limits, she didn't see a single soul. It was creepy.

Finally a massive ten-foot wall came into view up ahead. But the wall was just the beginning. The setting sun bathed the whole valley in a deep orange light, reflecting off the wall and the buildings inside it. The compound was set off the road, down a long driveway. This had to be Lucien's place. What else could it be? It was stunning!

In the center of the compound was a temple. It was a large, pyramidlike building made of stone and glass, which gave it a sort of ancient-yet-modern feel. Many buildings sprouted up around it, but the temple was the main attraction. From the size of the place, it looked like it could support several hundred people, no problem.

"Here goes nothing," Caylin muttered.

She took a deep breath and pedaled down the driveway to the main gate—two huge wooden doors that must have been barred from the inside. She saw no signs of life.

"Anybody home?" she whispered. She dismounted her bike, stretched, and walked toward the gate.

No doorbell. Oh, well. There was a small door cut into the gate at eye level. Caylin knocked on it.

Seconds passed. She heard nothing.

She knocked again.

Uh-oh, she thought. What kind of a lame spy would she be if she couldn't even get someone to answer the door!

Then as she raised her fist to knock again, the little square door popped open. A gruff-looking Asian man with a shaved head stared out at her. He said something she couldn't understand.

"Uh, hi!" she piped up in her best airhead English. "I'm from Omaha, Nebraska, and I'd like to see Luscious Lucien West, please!"

The man cocked an eyebrow and slammed the little door shut.

Great.

Caylin rapped on the door again. Harder this time. Time to go into Academy Award mode.

The same man's face appeared. Caylin waved dorkily.

"Uh, hi again. I don't think you understood me before," she said, tossing her long blond hair over her shoulder. "I'd like to come in. See, I

23

came all the way from Omaha, Nebraska, to see Luscious Lucien West. It would mean so much if you could just close that little door and open the big door so I can come in. Would that be okay?"

"Go eat a Big Mac, you silly American bimbo," the man growled.

Caylin's jaw dropped. "Bim . . . um, I'm sorry, but I could've sworn you just called me a *silly American bimbo*."

The man grinned. "Smart girl."

Caylin's eyes narrowed as she smiled back. "I thought so. Okay, then." She threw up her arms and turned back to her bike. "I guess I'll have to take all this cash somewhere else. Maybe to a casino in Thailand or something."

"Cash?" came the voice from the little door.

Gotcha.

Caylin turned around. "*Cash.* A donation for Lucien's cause. I'd really hoped to deliver it in person. I hear that this is the place to be, at least in this time zone."

The man leered, sizing her up. "Let me see."

Caylin smiled and unzipped a side pocket of her backpack. She pulled back the flap, exposing a thick wad of U.S. currency. Cold, hard cash.

The man's eyes widened. "Those hundreds?"

"Yeah. All I could get was the new ones, with the big Ben Franklin and his cheeks. But the banks in Switzerland didn't have any of the old ones. I dunno, these new bills are so hard to get used to. Don't you think?"

But the man was gone from the window.

Caylin quickly rezipped her backpack, put it back on, and tensed up, preparing for the worst. These people could do whatever they wanted out here in the middle of nowhere. Mug her. Rip her off. She had to be ready for anything.

But the big wooden doors only gave a loud thump.

Then they opened wide.

3

"I t really is a beautiful city," Theresa remarked as she and Jo made their way toward the waterfront.

She tilted back her head as a breeze lifted her hair from her neck and looked around. The town had everything a visitor could want, from restaurants to nightclubs to tour guides, all of them polished and open and friendly. But still, Kinh-Sanh was very much a country of the Orient, with traditional historic landmarks and a population that relied more on the bicycle than any other mode of transportation.

"It is beautiful," Jo agreed, hopping out of the way as a guy on a racing bike flew by. "But . . . I dunno."

"What?" Theresa asked.

"It just seems *too* nice," Jo replied, shrugging. "Like artificial nice. Even in the nicest parts of New York you still see the occasional homeless person. Not here. It almost seems too perfect. Like Disney World." She pointed to the street itself. "Check it out. No trash. Not even a cigarette butt. I mean, no place is *that* clean."

"That's a first," Theresa said with a laugh.

"What?"

"You're actually criticizing a place for being *too* nice."

"Very funny," Jo said, waving her off. "Which way's the warehouse?"

"We make a left at the next corner," Theresa replied, pointing. She gazed around her, noticing the locals passing by on their bikes. They would stare—but not so long as to be impolite. "Are we sticking out like the American sore thumbs that we are or what?"

"I know," Jo replied, leaning in close. "So much for being inconspicuous."

They made the left at the next corner. Within a few blocks the scenery started to change. Nightclubs became bars. Restaurants became tattoo parlors. And the average passerby became, well, more fragrant.

"Did you get a whiff of that guy with the beard?" Jo whispered, waving her hand in front of her nose. "Ugh!"

"Shhh," Theresa warned. "Remember—we're foreigners. You don't want to offend anyone."

"Then we shouldn't have showered," Jo replied, holding out her arms to show off her black Armani jacket and good taste. "We smell too good."

Theresa smirked. "You're a regular stand-up comedian."

As the sun set, the neighborhood gradually took on the odor of dead fish. Then the Spy Girls got their first glimpse of the harbor. Waves lapped against the docks, and buoy bells clanked out on the water. Massive cargo ships dominated the horizon, and seagulls battled over fish in midair.

"Is that the warehouse?" Jo asked, gesturing at a dark building that took up an entire block.

"It should be." Theresa nodded. "Let's check it out."

As they approached, Theresa noted that the area was strangely deserted. Maybe all the thirsty sailors had already found their dives of choice.

The warehouse loomed above. Most of the windows had wooden planks sloppily nailed over them. The bricks were grimy and weathered by the salt air, but the main doors of the place were recently repainted in a shiny green. Of course, the mondo padlock was shiny and new.

A gilded sign hung next to the main doors. In several languages it said: Future Site of the Lucien West Recreational Facility for Children.

"Awww, how sweet of him," Jo muttered.

"'Recreational facility,' huh?" Theresa scoffed. "We'll see about that."

* * *

29

The guard with the shaved head led Caylin across a huge courtyard. The compound was immaculate—from the new buildings surrounding the main temple, to the manicured lawns and gardens, to the gravel paths that crunched under their feet. All of it surrounded by a ten-foot stone wall topped with steel spikes.

Why would a religious sect need spikes on their wall? Caylin wondered. There didn't seem to be much riffraff to keep out. Was it to keep members in?

Before Caylin could decide, a girl approached her. She wore plain white pants and a matching long-sleeve shirt—almost like sweats, but perfectly clean. Little white slippers, too. Her light brown hair was pulled back from her face, and when she got close enough, Caylin saw that her eyes were jade green.

"Hi!" she said, shaking Caylin's hand. "I'm Jenny. Welcome to paradise."

"Paradise, huh?" Caylin replied, introducing herself and noting that Jenny was as American as apple pie. She was probably a cheerleader in a past life.

"You'll see," Jenny assured her. "You're American, too?"

Caylin nodded as Jenny took her by the arm and led her forward. The shaved-head guard disappeared. "I'm from Omaha. That's in Nebraska."

"I know. I'm from Bloomfield, Illinois," Jenny said with a sweet smile. "Which makes us practically neighbors."

Caylin grinned back. So, is Jenny the official hostess? she wondered. She seemed perfect for the job. There wasn't an inkling of stress in the girl's manner.

Caylin gazed in wonder at the layout. "This place is . . ."

"Amazing, yeah. You'll get to know your way around in no time. And you'll be so happy here. We all are."

Caylin blinked. "Really?"

"Don't sound so surprised," Jenny said with a laugh. She patted Caylin's arm gently. "You had to have been lost enough to want to find this place, right?"

"I guess so," Caylin said, casting down her gaze—as if to say that her whole life was meaningless up to this moment. "It took so long to get here."

"Well, you found us," Jenny replied softly. Her arm pat had become hand holding. "And I swear that you won't regret coming here, Caylin. Lucien has changed our lives."

Caylin gazed into Jenny's eyes, searching for sarcasm or insincerity. She found none. She means it. She really means it, Caylin thought.

Jenny sighed dreamily. "Before, it was all . . . I don't know, just one sleazy thing after another out there. I mean in the West. TV was depressing. Talk shows and *Seinfeld* repeats. School was depressing. Like, I wasn't learning anything, you know?"

"Believe me," Caylin replied earnestly. "I know."

Jenny nodded vigorously. "Yeah, it was all the same, right? I mean, what was I going to do when I got out of college? Go to work for some faceless corporation that wouldn't even pay me as much as a man in the same job? I had enough. I said 'when.'"

Caylin smiled. "I totally know what you mean. Coming to the Orient can be a life-altering experience. You see things a little differently. But I have to be honest. I do miss *Seinfeld* a little."

Jenny laughed. "That'll pass. Pretty soon you won't miss anything. The gardens and the mountains will be more than enough entertainment. And Lucien's gatherings are like the Super Bowl every week. You'll see."

"How many people are here?" Caylin asked, noting the perfect silence all around them.

"Seventy-two," Jenny declared proudly. "Everybody's from everywhere. The United States, Europe, Asia. The word is out on Lucien, and the quality of people is just great. I love them all. We're like a big family."

"Cool. I can't wait to meet them." And find out how brainwashed they are, Caylin thought.

"I've been here just over a year," Jenny

continued. "I'm sort of a senior member. I'll be your mentor during your indoctrination period. But feel free to ask any of the other members anything. There are no secrets here."

I'll be the judge of that, Caylin thought. "Sounds good to me."

Jenny nodded, then grinned a little too enthusiastically. "So . . . I hear that you have a small donation for the cause?"

Caylin grinned back. "Yeah," she replied, unshouldering her pack and unzipping the money pocket. She flashed the bills. "But I don't know. . . . Do you think it's enough?"

Jenny's slack jaw said it all. But she recovered nicely, smiling away. "I'm sure Lucien will be very grateful. Unfortunately money is a necessary part of what he's creating here. Without it we'd be treated as just another hippie cult. If you just give it to me, I'll make sure—"

"Actually," Caylin cut her off, closing the pack, "I was hoping to give this to him personally."

Jenny's expression darkened slightly, an abrupt shift. "Well . . . that's not usually how it's done."

"Oh, please, Jenny?" Caylin whined. "I came all this way. And if it's as great as everyone says it is, I can help out even more. I turned eighteen a few months ago, and I control my trust fund now. There'd be a lot more where this came from. I don't mean to be a skeptic, but I'm afraid that

Lucien is the one who will have to convince me."

"I don't know. . . . Lucien's a very busy man."

"*Pretty* please?" Caylin's tone was so sweet, she thought she might puke.

Jenny nodded reluctantly, then finally smiled. "I understand, Caylin. I'll see what I can do. Wait here."

"That padlock weighs more than my makeup kit," Jo grumbled. "Any ideas how we're going to open it?"

"Just one," Theresa replied, looking over her shoulder to make sure the alley was still deserted. The sun was quickly setting, and the light was growing rusty and dim. She slipped a hand inside a hidden pocket, pulled out her reading glasses, and put them on.

"You going to read me a bedtime story?" Jo asked.

"Did anyone ever tell you that you're too cynical, Jo?" Theresa asked, examining the lock.

"Let's see, um, only *everyone.*"

"Well, check this out, Miss Sarcasm." Suddenly twin red lasers shot out of Theresa's lenses. In seconds they burned through the steel clasp of the padlock. It burst open and clanked to the ground.

Theresa shut down the lasers and grinned at Jo.

"Holy Superman, Batman!" Jo marveled. "You have heat vision!"

"Just a little bit," Theresa replied, holding her thumb and index finger a smidgen apart.

"You sneak!" Jo exclaimed, whacking Theresa's arm. "How come Caylin and I didn't get glasses like those?"

Theresa shrugged. "Neither of you wear glasses. I need them to see my computer screen. Uncle Sam thought they might come in handy."

"Oh, that's fair. You're blind, so Cay and I get the shaft. Very nice."

"Shut your *boca*, girl. We have a warehouse to search. Or are you going to play the Spy Who Whined a Lot?" Theresa teased, raising an eyebrow.

"*Fine*," Jo growled, and opened the warehouse door. "But next time I'm requesting forty-four-magnum Gucci pumps."

The door creaked open, revealing a dark hallway. Jo and Theresa slipped inside and shut it behind them, plunging themselves in total darkness.

"I don't suppose you have little floodlights on your designer eyewear," Jo teased.

"You mean you didn't bring your flashlight?" Theresa muttered. She produced her own minilight. It was about the size of a cigarette lighter but very powerful. All the Spy Girls had one.

"I travel light," Jo replied indignantly.

"Too bad you don't travel flashlight," Theresa joked.

"You have absolutely no sense of style, Theresa, and it shows in your insults."

"Oh, rip my heart out, why don't you." Theresa shone the light at the far end of the dingy corridor. There was a rotted-looking door, peeling paint and all. "Come on."

They listened at the door but heard nothing. The hinges creaked angrily when they opened it, but no one seemed to be around to hear it. They found the main floor of the warehouse, a huge chamber half the size of a football field. It was big enough to hold an army of crates. And other than some splintered wood, foam peanuts, and rat droppings, it was empty.

"Yuck," Jo said, grimacing. "How about *that* smell?"

"Yep," Theresa replied, shining her light around. "That is definitely, without a doubt, a smell."

"And you call me a cynic," Jo muttered. "What now, Miss Dry Humor?"

"There are four or five more floors," Theresa suggested with a shrug.

Jo rolled her eyes. "Terrif."

The search continued, but all they found was more of the same—except for some live rats chittering in the corners. Which didn't make either Spy Girl very happy. They also found an office on the second floor. But other than cobwebs, a desk, and a rickety old chair, it had been picked clean.

They returned to the first floor, near a series of rusty garage doors that served as the main loading dock.

Theresa sighed. "Well, that's it."

"What about the basement?" Jo asked, delicately risking a seat on a crate.

"I don't think there is one," Theresa said. "There's no way down. Maybe the building's too close to the water to have a basement."

Jo picked a piece of warehouse grit from her perfectly pressed Calvin Klein jeans. "Who knows. What's the next move?"

Theresa shrugged. "I guess we head back to the flat. Hopefully my new laptop has arrived. I can take another hack at Lucien."

"And I can have a bath," Jo replied, wiping her hands on her sweet Armani sleeves.

They moved toward the front door, but something she saw out of the corner of her eye stopped Theresa. Something on the floor a few yards away. She shone the light.

It was a bright piece of cloth, decorated with an intricate red-and-yellow pattern.

"Hold up, Jo." Theresa picked it up and showed her partner. Jo reached out and held it between her forefinger and thumb, rubbing the fabric.

"It's silk," she said. "*Nice* silk."

"Look, it's cut into a sleeve pattern," Theresa

pointed out. "But it hasn't been sewn yet. Maybe they were storing textiles here."

"Yeah, and maybe it was left from the previous owner," Jo replied. "I mean, silk in the Orient isn't all that rare, right?"

"Right," Theresa said, dropping the sleeve. "I think I'm just clue happy. I'm starving—let's get some dinner."

They hit the street, checking first to see if anyone was lurking. The coast seemed clear. Theresa tossed what was left of the padlock into the harbor, and they walked briskly toward the tourist district.

"I wonder how Caylin's doing," Jo said, looking out at the water.

"Probably up to her black belt in peace and love," Theresa replied. "Hope she doesn't go crazy. I bet—"

A loud roar cut Theresa off. The Spy Girls whirled at the sound. And froze.

Four motorcycles squealed around the corner. Each was driven by a mystery figure clad in black leather from head to toe. As Theresa and Jo watched, stunned, the motorcycles stopped in a row and sat there, revving their engines ominously.

"Friends of yours from home?" Theresa whispered.

"Not me," Jo replied with a gulp. "Maybe we look like old girlfriends."

"That must be it," Theresa said, taking a tentative step back. "Who says romance is dead?"

"Romance . . . or *us?*"

The riders' leather seemed darker than Darth Vader's in the dim light. Their helmets covered their entire heads, and the visors were mirrored. But that wasn't the worst part.

Each rider carried a weapon. One had a baseball bat. Another had a pair of nunchaku—two lengths of wood attached by a thick chain. A third had a telescoping steel baton. And the last rider?

He slowly reached over his shoulder and unsheathed a razor-sharp samurai sword. He held the sword high and spun his wheels in place, kicking up a cloud of gray smoke.

"Uh, T. . . ."

"Yeah, Jo?" Theresa said, staring at the blade.

"I think we're in trouble."

With a loud screech of rubber, all four riders roared toward the Spy Girls!

4

aylin traced circles in the gravel with her toe. Jenny had been gone for a while, disappearing into the main temple. Caylin hoped that Uncle Sam had spotted her enough money to catch Luscious Lucien's eye. If not, she'd be stuck in this compound a very long time until she could get close to him.

Ha, Caylin thought. The almighty buck. You could buy your way into just about anything these days.

Off to her right small groups of "members" made their way from one building to another across the compound. Chow time? Maybe. This looked like a parade of the whole crew. They were dressed in the same simple white clothes as Jenny. And from what Caylin could see in the dim light, Jenny was right. All were about her age—yet all the faces were different. A true mix of nationalities from across the planet. Their manner was calm and leisurely. Their laughter genuine. They didn't have a care in the world.

Interesting.

Then Caylin caught sight of three men with shaved heads walking in a different direction.

Hmmm. More interesting.

Caylin wandered off the gravel path to get a better look at the men.

They were dressed differently than the members. Black robes. Very loose fitting. They were also much older than the members, and they all seemed so intense. Priests? Caylin doubted that. Yes, priests could be very intense, but this was a different kind of intensity. These men focused on what was going on *around* them, not inside them.

She'd only seen that kind of look in one other place—on the faces of the Secret Service types that she sometimes sparred with in the Tower gym.

Security. Yeah, that made sense. There sure was an army surplus of them. And the guy at the front gate was definitely rude enough.

Caylin felt a twinge of adrenaline. With that many guards around, she'd have to watch herself. . . .

"Hey," came a voice.

Caylin turned to see Jenny. Smiling as always.

"You weren't thinking of wandering off, were you?" she asked not so innocently.

Caylin smiled. "Not at all. I just wanted to get a better look at the sunset."

Jenny nodded. "You'll get some positively

amazing sunsets in these mountains. Enjoy them. We all do."

Of course you do, Caylin thought. No music, no gym, no TV. What else is there?

Jenny suddenly pulled Caylin close. "I have good news," she whispered. "Lucien has granted you an audience for a few brief moments."

"Awesome!" Caylin piped.

Jenny laughed and guided Caylin toward the main temple. "I know how you feel. I remember my first audience with Lucien. He's so . . . *in tune*, you know? It's like he can immediately read into your soul."

Hope not, Caylin thought, but forced herself to play up the breathless excitement. "Oh, I can't believe I'm actually going to meet him. Do I look okay?"

That was such a Jo thing to say, Caylin thought. Ugh.

"You'll do fine," Jenny reassured her. "Just be open and natural. Everything will take care of itself."

"O-okay."

When they got close to the large, ornate doors of the main temple, they swung inward like doors on an ultratacky Las Vegas supermarket. Caylin nearly burst out laughing.

But that feeling evaporated when she got a peek inside.

The ceiling had to be a hundred feet high.

Thick pillows for kneeling were lined up in a circle, surrounding a raised sofalike structure that was no doubt for Lucien. The walls were decorated in silver and gold, with an extensive collection of vases and sculpture throughout. She also noticed a pair of shaved heads hovering in the shadows. Caylin thought it odd that she was technically in a house of worship, but she saw no traditional religious trappings. She wondered exactly what Lucien and his followers worshiped.

"This is one of the main meditation chambers," Jenny whispered. "You'll eventually think of this place as your natural center. This is where all wrongs inside you become right again."

What*ever*, Jennifer, Caylin thought. This girl was just too placid for her. Caylin's natural center would forever be a gymnasium. But she had to play along. "It's beautiful, Jenny. I can't imagine a more perfect place."

"I told you so. We meet here as a group once a day in the morning. That way you can face your day without any questions. You always know where you belong."

Caylin leaned in close. "Where's Lucien?"

Jenny patted her hand. "Be patient. He'll be here soon. And then you can begin your new life."

Caylin tried to convey a desperate smile—as if to say that this place was her last hope. But she didn't want to overdo it. Jenny seemed so insanely happy, but how much was too much with these people? And what would happen if they figured out Caylin was a fake?

Suddenly a gong sounded.

Jenny stiffened. "It's time." She patted Caylin's hand once again and said, "Good luck." Then she retreated into the shadows.

Caylin whirled around. She didn't know which way to look. Then she spotted a set of double doors at the opposite end of the temple. With another deafening *gong*, the double doors slowly slid open.

She saw a silhouette, backlit by an intense floodlight. A tall, slim figure of a man. Flowing robes. Unearthly glow. An entrance fit for a king. The man stepped forward, and Caylin got her first good look at him. It was true. It was him.

Luscious Lucien West!

"Think it'll work if we play dead?" Theresa asked.

The motorcycles headed straight for them. The riders brandished their weapons, looking real ready to take the Spy Girls' heads off.

"That only works with grizzly bears!" Jo replied, shoving Theresa out of the way. "Look out!"

They split to each side of the alley, ducking between rusted garbage cans and mounds of junk. The cycles roared by, missing them by inches.

Jo and Theresa shared a look. This was serious.

The riders locked up their brakes fifty paces down the alley, stopping in a screech of burning rubber. They immediately turned the bikes around.

"What's the plan?" Theresa shouted to Jo.

"You're the smart one," Jo replied. "Talk to them."

"You're the flirt—*you* talk to them," Theresa yelled.

The bad guys gunned the engines once again and tore toward them. The weapons whirled above their heads—waiting to come down on the Spy Girls' own.

"I think hiding in the garbage is a bad idea!" Theresa hollered.

"I think you're *riiiiiighhht! Whoa!*"

The baseball bat came within inches of Jo's skull as the bikers raced by again. They screeched to a halt like before, but this time they were much closer. The Spy Girls had seconds to act.

"That's *it!*" Jo screamed. "That came very close to the hair!"

"What are you going to do?" Theresa asked desperately, watching in obvious horror as Jo stood up, grabbed a hunk of discarded wood, and marched defiantly to the middle of the alley. "Jo! Are you *nuts?*"

"Hey!" Jo called. "You! Yeah, you, the ugly one with the bat!" Jo brandished her own rickety club. "If you're so tough, why don't you come fight like a man!"

"Jo! He'll kill you!" Theresa pleaded.

"I'm defending myself," Jo replied angrily. "Just like the manual says I should."

"The manual didn't mention swords and bats!" Theresa shouted.

But it was too late. The rider with the bat came forward alone, responding to Jo's taunt. The other three stayed back, probably enjoying the show.

Jo planted her feet and took her best Mark McGwire batting stance—but instead of a pitcher, she faced another hitter. One with a real bat.

"C'mon, meat, show me the cheese!" Jo called.

The biker gunned the engine. The cycle lurched forward, gaining more speed. Jo held the club high. The rider held the bat higher. There was no way Jo could survive it. This was it. This Spy Girl had gone too far.

Jo wanted to close her eyes. But she couldn't.

It happened: impact.

But at the last second Jo crouched. The bat whizzed over her head, hitting nothing. Jo's club, however, hit home. She slammed it upward as the guy passed, catching him under the jaw. He flew off the back of the bike, his helmet spinning twenty feet in the air. He landed hard. The bat clattered. The helmet clunked down a second later. And the guy, bald head and all, lay there unconscious in front of them.

"Whoa," whispered Theresa. "Home run."

"Come on," Jo urged, tugging Theresa's sleeve.

"Where?"

Jo pointed at the guy's bike, which had continued on for a few yards, then pitched over on its side. Theresa's eyes widened. "No way!"

"You want to stay with them?" Jo said, pointing to the now advancing bikers. "Be my guest."

Such a scummy individual doesn't deserve such a fine motorcycle, anyway, she thought excitedly. I'm riding this beautiful machine all the way home.

Jo grabbed the handlebars and mounted the bike, muttering machine specs as she went: "The MRZ 669, German made, top street speed 188, equipped with the Floydian Model 2 motor cross tires. . . . T., get the lead out!"

Theresa stared at the bike revving beneath Jo, shaking her head. "I can't do this, Jo. I *can't.*"

Behind them the other bikes swooped in.

"Theresa."

She reluctantly met Jo's stare.

"Trust me."

Theresa glanced back at the approaching riders and hopped on behind Jo. "You're just lucky I don't have any other choice."

"I hope there's enough luck for both of us," Jo shouted above the revving engines. "Hang on!"

Jo peeled out, Theresa lurched, and the chase was on!

Lucien's some on.....: "I want you to feel at welcome here" .... anywhere.

"Thank you .... but I know how happy it makes .... I've been so .... until .... I've ...."

Lucien's expression turned to concern. He put a hand on .... shoulder and quieted her.

"Walk with me, Caylin," he said earnestly, slow ......

Lucien West stepped forward from the doorway and strode toward Caylin. He walked with total confidence: slowly, deliberately. As if to let whoever was there know that no matter what room he entered, it immediately became *his* room.

He wore an intricate mass of white robes, with a tan top robe that would have seemed silly on anyone else. But Lucien pulled it off. He looked almost regal: black hair cut close, coming to a pronounced widow's peak over a strong brow ... blue eyes, deep-set but piercing, focused at all times on Caylin ... smooth, close shave. His smile widened as he approached.

"Caylin," he greeted her, enveloping her hand in both of his. His handshake was firm and warm. "Welcome to our sanctuary. I've heard so much about you that I feel we've already met."

"Hello, Mr. West," Caylin said breathlessly. "It's so nice to finally meet you. I've come such a long way."

"Yes, we all have. But you're home now, Caylin."

Lucien's voice was deep, soothing. "I want you to feel as welcome here as you ever have anywhere."

"Thank you," she said. "You don't know how happy it makes me to hear that. I've been so . . . I dunno . . . lost, I guess."

Lucien's expression turned to concern. He put a hand on Caylin's shoulder and guided her. "Walk with me, Caylin," he said earnestly, slowly strolling around the perimeter of the temple. "I know how lost you must feel. I was, too. So lost. Every day faded into the next. I had no purpose. Everyone around me seemed determined to hold me back or bring me down to their level. It hardly seemed fair. Is that what you're feeling?"

Caylin nodded. "It's like a twenty-ton weight on my shoulders. It took all the courage I had just to find my way here."

"Jenny says you're from Nebraska," Lucien said, sounding sincerely interested.

"Yeah, Omaha." She chuckled. "There's not a lot going on in Omaha."

"I can imagine."

Caylin gazed up into Lucien's face. His eyes locked on to hers and held them. Beautiful blue eyes. Crystal clear. Honest. Understanding. It was as if he truly wanted to know what was going on in her heart and soul. Caylin thought she was putting on a pretty good act. But if Lucien was acting . . . well, he deserved to be right up there with De Niro.

What if Lucien was exactly what he said he was? What if this whole Carruthers thing was just a case of mistaken identity?

"You see, Caylin," Lucien said, holding her gaze, "it takes a long time to realize that where you stand on the planet really has nothing to do with where you are emotionally and spiritually."

"I'm not sure I understand," Caylin said.

"Well, someone who lives in Omaha who is perfectly happy with who they are probably thinks that it's the most wonderful place on the planet." He placed his hand against his chest. "Inside affects outside, you see?"

Caylin nodded. "I think so."

Lucien smiled and placed his hands on Caylin's shoulders. His ice blue eyes were clearer than ever. Enveloping her.

"That's mostly what we do here, Caylin. The people who come to me are lost like you. But that doesn't mean they're worthless, or useless, or cast aside. It just means they're lost. And when you find yourself, you'll come to think of this place as home. You belong here, Caylin. I can tell. You definitely belong here with us. . . ."

Caylin stared into Lucien's eyes. She saw nothing there that hinted at ill will or evil or whatever Uncle Sam was accusing him of. Lucien did this because he cared. Caylin, at that moment, was sure of it.

51

His eyes were so beautiful. . . .

She couldn't help staring into them. Couldn't help listening to the calmness of his voice as he made everything seem so much better. The grounds were peaceful, the surrounding country-side beautiful and calming.

This place really is a utopia, Caylin thought.

And Lucien was the perfect guide to its spiritual treasures.

But that's why he's so good at what he does, she thought, suddenly feeling very tired. The jet lag and the bike ride were catching up with her. . . .

So good . . . so very, very good . . .

The alleys zipped by at a speed too terrifying to consider. Jo was too busy driving to look. And Theresa was too busy cringing to care.

"Are they still there?" Jo called.

"What?" Theresa shouted.

"Are they still there? I don't have mirrors!"

"I'm not looking!" Theresa's eyes were squeezed shut.

"You have to look!" Jo demanded.

Theresa shook her head. "No way!"

"Way! Just look, for crying out loud!"

Theresa was frozen, but she forced herself to glance behind them. She was convinced that any movement on her part would send the bike into a violent spin and kill the both of them. But nothing happened.

Until the samurai sword sliced down into the taillight of their bike!

The red plastic shattered, spilling out behind them. The swordsman—mere inches off their back end—raised the blade for another strike.

"Are they still there?" Jo called.

"Yeah, they're still there! Gun it!" Theresa screamed.

Jo hammered the throttle, and the samurai sword swished open air.

Theresa's panic suddenly turned to red-hot anger. She pulled closer to Jo and yelled, "I've had it with these animals! Get us out of here!"

"Just lean into the turns more," Jo ordered. "This could get ugly."

Theresa nodded and tried to concentrate on the road. But it wasn't a road. It was a back alley in the seediest part of a foreign city. Filled with crates, Dumpster containers, and cargo trucks hauling fish.

In other words, lots to hit.

The bike swerved between debris. Theresa's stomach churned. Jo must have been hoping to catch one of the other riders in a mistake. But it didn't happen. They stayed a few feet off their tail, trying to maneuver into position for the killing strike.

"Time for something different," Jo said.

She swerved suddenly. Theresa thought her heart would come up her throat. She clamped her arms around Jo and tried to lean with her. The back tire of the bike kicked out with the swerve, slamming into a large stack of crates. The whole thing came down with a crash.

Theresa glanced behind them just in time to see the biker with the steel baton go flying over his handlebars and into a mass of rusty trash cans.

"Got one!" Theresa cheered.

The other two bikers seemed to take it personally. They revved and closed the distance between them in seconds. Jo wove in and out of more garbage and obstacles, trying desperately to stay in front of the men in black. But this was their town. They knew the alleys.

The biker with the nunchaku closed in. His front tire brushed Theresa's right foot, flinging it out in an involuntary kick. Panic gripped her and she screamed. In a terrifying instant she turned, saw the blur coming at her head, and lashed out in self-defense.

She screamed again. Blinding pain shot up her arm. Did the nunchaku hit her?

Then she saw it.

They hadn't hit her. *She'd caught them in mid-strike!*

Her hand gripped the business end of the

weapon without her even knowing it. Now she and Jo were towing the other biker. He yanked back, but Theresa held on, playing a vicious tug-of-war.

"What's happening?" Jo called out.

The alley widened, allowing the biker to move up alongside Jo and Theresa. Now the nunchaku were pulled tight between the two bikes. Theresa refused to let go, yanking back harder every time the bad guy tried to pull her off the bike. They wobbled dangerously on each tug.

"Are you crazy, T.—let go!" Jo ordered.

But Theresa couldn't. Her hand was locked on, and there was nothing she could do about it.

Suddenly Jo saw something up ahead. She immediately swerved into the other biker. He instinctively swerved away, still holding the nunchaku tight between them like some unbreakable bridge.

Then he screamed, seeing what Jo had seen— a loading dock ramp.

Jo swerved away and the biker rolled up the ramp, letting go of the nunchaku just as he took to the air.

He flew off his bike, screaming, arms pinwheeling, until the whole mess came down in a massive bin of dead fish.

The Spy Girls roared on, Jo laughing, Theresa holding the dangling nunchaku in her aching hand.

Before they could relax, the last biker—sword in hand—closed in.

"Lean!" Jo hollered, taking a wicked left turn. The bike skidded beneath them, nearly spilling them all over the pavement. But they held their balance and rolled on. Up ahead Theresa could see the harbor and water.

The sword slammed down into Theresa's seat—less than an inch from her back!

That was too close! A fresh surge of adrenaline went through her, and she lashed out with the nunchaku. They clattered against the steel of the sword, causing no damage. Theresa got a good look at the rider, the folds of his leather, the sheen of his mirrored visor. Faceless. Evil.

He raised the sword again, prepared to cut the head right off her shoulders.

Fear gripped her.

She actually caught sight of the razor edge, the line of surgical steel that would cut right through her body.

It was almost like a strange hypnosis. . . . Theresa could see the blow coming but could do nothing to stop it.

Suddenly the bike lurched again, making yet another left, away from the swordsman.

But he kept going straight.

Right into the harbor.

The bike slammed into a thick cement pylon,

sending the biker and his sword spinning out over the water. The bike exploded in a spray of flames and steel chunks. The guy flipped over and over again and finally splashed down.

"He's gone!" Theresa blurted out. "We got them all!"

"Yeeeeeehaaaaa!" Jo cried at the top of her lungs. She gunned the engine in exultation.

Warehouses whizzed by on one side, the harbor on the other. The exhilaration of victory gripped Theresa as they cheered and laughed . . .

. . . until a large panel truck pulled out in front of them!

The Spy Girls screamed.

There was no way to stop!

Caylin shook her head suddenly. Blinked. What just happened?

Lucien still stared at her. "Are you okay, Caylin?"

"Yeah," she said, nodding, trying to clear her head. "It's just been a very long trip."

"Yes, of course. You must be exhausted," Lucien said in a kind voice.

Caylin smiled wanly. She couldn't believe what just happened to her. Lucien had tried to use some kind of hypnosis! Powerful stuff, too. Caylin Pike swooned for no man, no matter how (literally) hypnotic they were. She wasn't about to start now.

But still, she had to keep up a good front. She had to look like she was buying into his spiel—without truly falling under his spell. She had to keep focused, no matter what.

"Now, Caylin," Lucien said gently. "I understand you have something for me."

Caylin smiled and nodded. "Yes, I do." She went to her pack and pulled out five thick stacks of hundred-dollar bills. She handed them over to him—the first time that Lucien's eyes didn't lock on to hers.

Guess he sees something more interesting, she thought sarcastically.

"Sorry it's not wrapped or anything," she said lamely. "It seems . . . I dunno, kind of tacky just handing you a pile of cash."

"Nonsense," Lucien assured her. "Donations can come in all forms, Caylin. And this particular donation is quite generous. Thank you."

He somehow slid all five stacks of cash into his robe. Caylin wondered just how many inside pockets he had.

Caylin grinned, showing how happy she was to please him. "Um, I don't want to seem too pushy, Mr. West—"

"Call me Lucien, Caylin," he said with a smile.

"Okay. Lucien. But if this works out for me—and I'm not saying it won't or anything . . ."

"Of course not," Lucien reassured her.

". . . I can help out even more. With the money, I mean. I have a trust fund and—"

"Caylin, Caylin." Lucien stopped her. "Don't worry about that now. There will be plenty of time for that. Right now I want you to concentrate on your inner self. You must relax and find what you have lost. Do you understand?"

Caylin offered up a sheepish grin. "Yeah, I understand. Sorry for being too eager."

"That's fine. You're not in Omaha anymore. Here you have all the time in the world," Lucien said, gesturing grandly at the room around them. "Here you'll find what was lost. Call it what you want. Peace, harmony, enlightenment. Freedom from a bankrupt culture that values HDTV, DVD, and SUV. If you ask me, there's not enough LUV. I want you to think about that. Relax. Let nature take her course. You'll see. I promise you."

Caylin nodded. Boy, he talked the talk and walked the walk, didn't he? But Caylin wondered if this man was capable of true evil.

It was anyone's guess.

But she knew she was the only one who could find out for sure.

Jo jammed on the brakes and turned the bike sideways, spilling herself and Theresa onto the pavement. They flopped and rolled with the momentum, trying to shield their heads and faces.

The bike slid on, slamming into the rear tires of the truck.

The Spy Girls rolled to a stop, and Jo deliriously watched as the truck crunched over the remains of the bike. The driver stopped, got out of the truck, and surveyed the smoking wreckage. Then he started waving his arms and screaming obscenities in Kinh-Sanhian.

"Whoa," Jo moaned, rolling over.

"Beyond whoa," Theresa croaked, holding a bleeding elbow.

"You okay?" Jo asked, grimacing when she saw T.'s wound.

"I'll live . . . I think," Theresa muttered. "Where did you learn how to parallel park?"

"Now we're criticizing my driving?"

All Theresa could do was laugh. Jo scowled and then finally joined in.

"So, Caylin," Lucien said with a smile. "You've had a small introduction to our little section of the world here. But I'd like to discuss it further with you if that would be okay?"

"Okay?" Caylin gushed. "That would be great!"

"Splendid. I know you must be very tired from your journey, so take some time to clean up and get settled. Jenny will see to you. After that, I was hoping you would join me for a late supper in my quarters."

Uh-oh, she thought. Is this a date?

Caylin kept up her act, however, looking thrilled. "I'd *love* to, Lucien. It's more than I ever could have hoped for on my first day."

"It's the least I can do," Lucien replied. But he paused when he spotted a shaved head approaching. "Excuse me, Caylin. Just for a moment."

He met the bald man and spoke to him in hushed tones. The man looked incredibly intense, his brow furrowed and his jaw set.

Then Caylin saw it—Lucien's visage turned to rage for a split second. Not displeasure or impatience. But rage. Something the man said truly ticked him off. And Caylin knew that the face that had been so calming and handsome could be just as frightening. Lucien's personality was incredibly powerful—in both extremes.

Finally Lucien dismissed the shaved head. He stood for a moment with his back to Caylin, composing himself. He straightened his robe, took a deep breath, and turned back to her.

He was all serene smile. "I apologize for the interruption, Caylin."

"Is something wrong?" she asked innocently.

"Not at all," Lucien replied with a wave of dismissal. "I believe we were discussing dinner?"

"Yeah, it sounds too good to be true!" Caylin gushed, even going so far as clapping excitedly. Lucien stared at her hands.

For a split second panic gripped her—she'd gone too far. The clapping was *way* over the top.

But Lucien simply grinned at her enthusiasm.

"Wonderful!" he exclaimed. "It's settled. When it's time, you'll be called. Until then, I hope you're comfortable."

"I'm sure I will be. Thanks so much, Lucien. It means the world."

He smiled in total confidence. "Your world, Caylin, is about to change dramatically. Both our worlds are. The worlds in here"—he touched his head and chest—"and the real world that surrounds us all." His eyes grew sparkly and playful and—Caylin was sure of it—a little sinister. "The world is ripe for a colossal change . . ."

Lucien's grin intensified.

". . . and I, beautiful Caylin, am going to make that happen."

Jo and Theresa returned to the flat in peace. And pieces.

Actually, besides some scrapes and cuts—a particularly nasty one on Theresa's elbow—they were basically okay. But when she looked in the mirror inside the front door, all Theresa could see were two girls buried under a layer of dirt, grease, and fish oil.

"So how many lives do you have left?" Jo asked as they limped into the living room. "I think this cat's down to about three."

"And we were worried that we were too clean," Theresa grumbled in reply.

Jo ripped her once beautiful Armani jacket off and threw it across the room in disgust. "I can't believe those slimeballs totaled my jacket! Do you know how long it took me to find a tailor who could press it just right?"

"About as long as it's going to take me to strangle you," Theresa replied wearily. "I can hardly lift my arms . . . but in your case, I'll make an exception."

Jo glared at her. "Hey, I got us out of there. And we're the ones still walking."

"You call that walking?" Theresa said of Jo's exhausted limp. "You look like Yoda trying to be a runway model."

"Oh, shut up."

She and Jo shuffled in and slumped down on the throw pillows. After a few minutes of exhausted silence, they had enough energy to get up for some beverages and food. But the throw pillows were like magnets. Soon they were lounging again, listening to the hustle and bustle on the street outside. Staring at the exotic nighttime skyline through the long windows that lined the far wall.

"Is it me," Theresa said, "or was that attack a little too smooth to be a random run-in with a bike gang?"

"That was a professional hit," Jo replied. "No doubt about it. Those MRZ bikes are too pricey for your average hood. They're racing bikes. They start in the mid-five-figure range." She smirked. "And oh, what a treat to ride."

Theresa fished an ice cube out of her soda and held it against a bruise on her forehead. She winced. "Then we are definitely on to something. Do you think the warehouse is a front?"

Jo shrugged. "For what? It's empty."

"Empty. Yet guarded by killer bikers," Theresa pointed out.

Jo sighed and rubbed her sore back. "Nothing adds up."

"Well, let's try some of that math," Theresa offered. "Between the warehouse and my poor nuked computer, you have a second-rate cult leader who wears high security like a bullet-proof vest."

"But for what?" Jo pressed. "Bilking rich college kids out of their inheritances?"

"It has to be something bigger." Theresa shook her head slowly. "You're talking about attempted murder and government-level encryptions. Not to mention four brand-new MRZ motorcycles. That's some slick financing. That tells me Lucien's not so second-rate."

"Great," Jo grumbled. "And as usual, we don't know squat."

Theresa rolled over and gazed grimly at her partner. "Whatever it is, Jo, we better find out soon. Because our best friend is right in the middle of it."

After receiving Lucien's gracious invitation to dinner, Caylin was turned over to Jenny, who showed Caylin to her quarters. Outwardly Jenny was still just as friendly, but Caylin immediately noticed a chillier air from her.

"Lucien has never done that before," Jenny pointed out as they crossed the compound to the members' quarters.

"Done what?" Caylin asked.

"Asked a new arrival to have dinner with him—in *his* quarters." Jenny smiled slyly. "You must have made quite an impression."

Caylin shrugged. "I'm just going with the flow."

They crossed the courtyard and entered a stone building. Jenny led her to the second floor and down a long hallway that resembled a college dorm. She opened a door about halfway down the hall and flipped on the light. Inside was a bed, already made, a desk and chair, and a small closet. A set of white garments was laid out on the bed for her.

"I guessed at the size," Jenny said as Caylin lifted her white top from the mattress. "I hope they fit."

"I'm sure it will be fine," Caylin replied. They're so baggy they might as well be one size fits all, she thought.

"Everyone gets their own room," Jenny said. "Everything you'll need is provided for you. Someone will come along and take your backpack."

Caylin paused. "They will?"

"Don't worry. All our personal belongings are put into storage, but you have access to them anytime you want to. But believe me, after a while you'll forget you ever brought anything with you." Jenny chuckled. "I haven't gone through my stuff in about four months."

Wow, Caylin thought. She's truly let it all go. I wonder what Jenny was like before she got here.

Caylin smiled at her. "This place really is your home."

Jenny smiled back. "It's hard to remember what life was like before I came to Lucien's world. Yes, it really is home."

Caylin dumped her pack on the bed and sat down, glancing around the nearly bare room. She couldn't believe that people actually lived without stimulus from the outside world. She'd go nuts without her workouts, her sparring, and the occasional cheesy Jean Claude Van Dammage flick. Thankfully, this arrangement was temporary. But she still had to keep up a solid front.

"If you want to take a shower, the shower room is down the hall," Jenny said before leaving. "It's expected that you wear the whites for your first audience with Lucien. First official audience, that is."

"Thanks," Caylin said. "A shower sounds good."

Ha, she thought, that's the first honest thing I've said since I got here.

"Good luck, Caylin," Jenny said, her hand on the doorknob. "You can meet the others tomorrow. Until then, enjoy what Lucien has to say."

"He's very charming, isn't he?" Caylin said, looking Jenny in the eye.

Jenny couldn't suppress her grin. "Lucien is . . . *everything*, Caylin. It's the only way to describe him. You'll see. Good night."

"Good night," Caylin said with a wave.

Jenny closed the door without a sound.

Whoa. That girl is either seriously programmed or has a serious crush . . . or both, Caylin thought.

She prepped for her shower. But before leaving the room, she slipped the tiny Tower cell phone out of her backpack and carried it with her. She wasn't going to call the Spy Girls just yet, but she didn't want the phone out of her sight until she could find a safe hiding place for it.

It was a good thing, too. For when she returned from her shower, her backpack—including all of her personal effects—was gone. Creepy. She donned the white vestments, which proved to be quite comfortable.

A few minutes later a shaved head came to her door.

It was time for dinner.

The guard—Caylin couldn't help but think of the shaved heads as guards—led her back across the compound to the main temple. But this time she was led to the far side, behind a curtain and down a long hall. At the end was an open elevator. The guard gestured for her to get in.

When she did, the door shut and she shot upward. The ride was brief. As far as Caylin could tell, she was on the top floor of the temple building.

The doors opened, and she stepped out into paradise, part two.

68

Lucien's private quarters were breathtaking. A twenty-foot-long window stretched from floor to ceiling all around them, offering a view of the compound and surrounding mountains that was worth a stack of cash.

The center of the room was sunk into the floor, with three steps leading down into it. This was the dining area, apparently. The table was round but with short little legs. They would have to squat on pillows to eat. The smell of oriental cooking wafted to her, and immediately Caylin's stomach growled. She'd forgotten that she hadn't eaten all day.

"Caylin," came Lucien's voice.

She turned, and there he was. He must have come out from behind one of the many curtains that lined the wall behind her. He still wore his white robes but had dumped the tan one. Leisure wear, Caylin mused.

"So . . . do you approve of the view?" he asked.

"It's amazing," Caylin replied. "Leadership sure has its privileges."

Watch it, she warned herself. That comment sounded a little too much like the real Caylin. She had to be more lame and humble.

But Lucien laughed at the quip. "It certainly does. I find this place so peaceful. It grounds me. And reminds me that even though I act as mentor to many people, I'm still just a simple man. The mountains out there are a lot bigger than I am."

That's funny, Caylin thought. An hour earlier he was talking about being the one who would change the world.

Lucien approached her and felt the fabric of her sleeve. He smiled. "These suit you, I think. Are they comfortable?"

Caylin tried not to squirm. As handsome and charming as he was, she didn't like him being so close.

"Yeah. It's nice not to have to think about what to wear to dinner," Caylin said.

Lucien chuckled. "One of the many advantages of simple clothing is lack of distraction." He gestured at the table. "Shall we eat?"

"Yeah, I'm starving."

They sat down at the table. Caylin imitated Lucien, tucking her legs underneath her. It wasn't very comfortable. What she wouldn't have given for a regular old kitchen chair and a real table.

They dined on an exotic variety of local dishes. Noodles, fish, root vegetables, and a very bitter tea. "Decaffeinated, of course," Lucien said with a smile.

"Of course," Caylin replied, hoping he wasn't drugging her. After that hypnotic episode, she wasn't trusting this guy any further than she could throw his bankbook. She tried to get him to talk—which wasn't a problem. Lucien seemed to like the sound of his own voice. "So how did you start this?"

Lucien took a sip of tea. "I was like you, Caylin. Lost," he said, replacing his cup on the table. "Wandering the world from place to place, looking for something that meant something. You know, as different as each country in the world can be, they are all basically the same. The East, the West, virtually anywhere you go—you work for money and material gain. You try to find a job that is somehow fulfilling. But most people just find something they can tolerate. So you can have the beautiful apartment, the 'phat flat,' so to speak."

This made him chuckle, and Caylin did, too. Politely.

"Then what?" Lucien continued. "Start a family? Work even harder. To what end? Most jobs break your back and your heart. When I got here, I found this compound. It was an old temple that was just falling apart. The local government had no interest in it, so I took what money I had left and I bought it." He smiled, and his eyes grew distant. "You have no idea how that one act changed my life. It was as if I suddenly took control of everything. As if I finally grabbed the helm of my own life and started steering. Soon others started to come. We'd talk, and they'd find that they were just like me. All they had to do was take control and steer their own course. I helped them do that. Now there are over seventy people here. We've built something that's not only beautiful but meaningful."

Caylin honored his long speech with a moment of reverent silence—it seemed appropriate.

"That's amazing," Caylin said finally. "You make it sound so easy."

"It is!" Lucien said, his beautiful eyes sparkling. "All you have to do is take the last step. You know in your heart what's always been the problem. Now you're here. Take the step."

She smiled shyly. "This is a little weird for me. I mean, no one ever told me I was ever good enough to accomplish anything." As she said the words, she thought about how sad they sounded and was suddenly glad she hadn't led the type of life that would actually force her to come here for help.

Lucien stared deep into her eyes, his expression both passionate and sympathetic. "It's time to leave all that behind, Caylin. Here you can accomplish anything you desire. You just have to let yourself."

They stared at each other for a few intense moments. Caylin felt the hypnotic trance creeping in again, and she fought it off. She blinked and looked away.

Lucien smiled and sipped his tea. "I hope you

decide to stay for a while, Caylin. Things are only going to get more exciting. I have many plans."

Caylin's ears perked up at this. "Really?"

He nodded. "*Big* plans. I hope to help beautify this whole country. I've been dealing closely with the prime minister himself. He's seen what I've done with this site. In fact, he sat exactly where you're sitting and told me how impressed he is."

"That's amazing, Lucien."

"Yes, it is pretty impressive. It wasn't something I expected. But we've struck up a spiritual partnership, so to speak."

"A partnership?" Caylin prodded.

"Absolutely," Lucien replied earnestly. "I want to expand and help beautify the country the way I have this place. I want to help the children of Kinh-Sanh as well. I have plans for a large recreational center in the capital city."

"Really?" Caylin asked, faking breathlessness.

Lucien nodded, smiling. "Yes, it's really going to be wonderful. Eventually I want to build a spiritual retreat in the capital city that is even larger than this one. Sort of a playground for the enlightened. After that, I'm even thinking about franchises."

Caylin's eyes widened. "Wow. Franchises?" Kentucky Fried Enlightenment? she thought.

"Why not? Why should this kind of paradise be restricted to Kinh-Sanh? There are so many places that would benefit from what we have here. It's definitely—"

He paused, looking over Caylin's shoulder. She turned.

A grim-looking shaved head was motioning for Lucien.

"Excuse me, Caylin," Lucien said calmly. "I won't be but a moment."

He stood and trotted over to the bald man. They conferred briefly, and then Lucien followed the man to one of the curtains in the corner.

Then they disappeared behind it.

Adrenaline surged through Caylin. She needed to find out what was back there. From how Lucien was talking, he was a spiritual emperor waiting to happen. That wasn't necessarily evil, but the ambition in this man was not to be taken lightly. *Franchises?*

She looked around. No other guards, as far as she could see. She quickly and gracefully covered the distance to the curtain. She smiled, so happy that she was able to *move* again. She paused, listening.

No sound.

Wait—

She heard low talking.

Between the curtains Caylin could see a sliver of light. Did she dare peek through? What if she was caught?

Well, she could just say she was looking for the bathroom. That always seemed to work. She was new here, after all. An innocent. At least, she was trying to put up that front. She assumed Lucien believed her. The little naive girl from the Midwest.

She could plead innocence. Sorry, Lucien. I just didn't know any better.

That was the ticket.

Excitement boiled within her. She reached up to the curtain. Pinched it gently. Pulled it slightly. The sliver of light grew larger.

Caylin took a deep breath . . . and peeked through.

"Maybe that silk sleeve meant something," Theresa wondered aloud. She sipped her soda and winced as her hurt elbow gave her a jolt of pain. "It was the only thing tangible in the whole building."

"You mean other than splinters and rat poops," Jo replied. She rolled onto her back and stared at the ceiling. "Sorry, T., I don't buy it. What would a possible nuke smuggler want with high-end silk? I think we're so desperate for a clue that we'll consider anything at this point."

"I hate it when you're right," Theresa muttered.

"Then you must hate just about everything I say, huh?" Jo quipped.

Theresa burst out laughing. "Yeah, you just keep on believing that, Jo. Then it must be true."

"Oh, it's true," Jo said, smiling slyly.

"Whatever. I think we owe it to ourselves to let Uncle Sam in on all this."

Jo nodded. "Good idea. He might have a helpful hint."

Theresa wrinkled her nose. "Helpful? Sammy? All he ever does is bark at us. It's like he's a demented parent and high-level civil servant all rolled into one."

"You're being too hard on the old guy," Jo said. Her eyes narrowed playfully. "I bet he's hot."

Theresa looked horrified. "Uncle Sam? Are you nuts?"

"Come on," Jo protested. "That voice, that authoritarian manner. I bet he's a handsome man."

Theresa shook her head. "No way. I think he hides behind that digital distortion because he looks like the Phantom of the Opera."

"Look at *Charlie's Angels*," Jo argued. "Charlie turned out to be Blake Carrington, this totally sexy billionaire."

Theresa rolled her eyes. "Charlie turned out to be the *voice* of John Forsythe, a handsome character actor who *played* a billionaire on TV. I think you're taking your spy fantasy just a little too far. And another thing, the flat is probably bugged. Uncle Sam now knows that you have a crush on him."

Jo's jaw dropped. "I do not!"

"What did you just say?" Theresa asked, grinning. "Two key words: hot and sexy."

Jo shook her head violently and turned her voice up several decibels. "If you're listening, Sammy, *I do not have a crush on you.* T.'s making the whole thing up. She's bored since she broke her computer."

"Very nice, Jo. Now you're talking to walls."

Jo sank back into her pillows. "As long as they don't answer me."

"Anyway, we still should call Uncle Sam. I need to remind him that the encryptions on my new computer need to be top-shelf." Theresa's jaw ground at the thought of being hoodwinked by another programmer. "With this new gear I'll be able to hack into Bill Gates's pocket protector. No huckster hacker is going to keep me out of Luscious's files."

She smiled a deliciously evil smile.

"His little empire is coming down."

Caylin gasped as she peeked between the curtains.

It was a computer room!

The entire right wall was a complex system of

spinning, humming, clicking hard drives. An air conditioner blew frigid air from the ceiling. Several bald techies pecked away on various keyboards or pulled apart circuit boards.

A few feet away Lucien and the man who must have been the head techie were having a heated discussion.

"You have to understand, Mr. West," he said firmly—placatingly. "No files were compromised. All information is intact."

"How were they able to break in as far as they did in the first place?" Lucien demanded, his blue eyes flashing.

The techie shrugged. "They were very good." He smiled in satisfaction. "We were better."

Lucien smiled back sarcastically. "You were better. Yet you weren't good enough to track this thief down. I need to know where they are if I'm to prevent this from happening again."

"I can tell you that whoever hacked in was an expert," Baldie explained, glaring at the computers. "They left no trail. No footprints. But our security programs are quite vicious. The culprits won't be back anytime soon unless they have access to another machine with the same power." He grinned. "They got nuked in a big way. Their machines wouldn't even be able to tell them the date and time."

Caylin smiled. They *had* to be talking about

Theresa. She must be furious that they nuked her precious laptop!

Suddenly Lucien got in the man's face, pointing a threatening finger. "You listen to me, Max. If this happens again, I don't just want their computers nuked. I want their location. Do you understand me? These security breaches stop immediately."

Max nodded his bald head. "I understand. But I need to upgrade the programming. The CIA has some new encryptions that will help. But it'll take some cash. And some contacts."

"You do whatever you have to do to make those files safe," Lucien warned. "No one, but no one, must know of my plans. If they find out, we're all out of business."

Lucien turned toward the curtain.

Caylin sprinted back to the table. She hurdled a cushion and the three steps down to land right where she had been sitting before.

Lucien walked out and took a moment to straighten his robes. Then he calmly strode back to his seat.

Caylin smiled at him and sipped her tea. Her cheeks were red-hot, but in this light she didn't think Lucien would notice.

"Now, beautiful Caylin," he said brightly. "Where were we?"

Caylin grinned, primed for more info. "Franchises!"

The morning light blasted through the tall windows of the flat. Jo emerged from her room fully dressed and ready to take on the world if need be.

"Yo, T.!" she called.

"In here," Theresa replied.

Jo found her in the computer room, pecking away on a new laptop. The machine was also hooked into a strange square black box. Theresa's glasses had slid down her nose, and her hair was a snakelike mass. Her flannel pj's and T-shirt were rumpled.

"What's with you?" Jo asked.

Theresa didn't look up from her work. "The computer got here about four in the morning. I couldn't wait to hook it up."

Jo looked at her watch. "You've been sitting there for *six hours?*"

Theresa scratched her head. "I dunno. You tell me."

"Okay. You've been sitting there for six hours.

Don't you want to get out for a while?" Jo suggested.

"Not a chance." She furiously typed away. "I've got this sucker on the run. I can feel it." She patted the black box next to her. "This little puppy can wreak more havoc than a Death Star run by Dennis the Menace."

Jo rolled her eyes. "Well, I'm not going to sit around all day watching you type. I'm heading out for a walk. Do you think maybe we can save the world or something tonight? If the rest of this adventure is all cyberstalking, I'm going home."

Theresa typed and typed. Her answer was distant, as if she didn't even hear herself speaking. "Sure, okay."

Why do I bother? Jo wondered. She threw up her arms and left.

Once on the street, Jo headed toward the market district they'd passed through on the rickshaw ride in. The city was bustling. People on bicycles darted in and out of slow-moving traffic. Tourists aimed their cameras and said *"fromage."* And the whole place generally went about its business.

The market district was about a twenty-minute walk. Once Jo got there, it was unmistakable. The smell of spiced noodles was overpowering. The temperature seemed to rise as the quarters suddenly got very close. Everyone was pushed together, shuffling between rickety tables and drab tents. The tourists didn't look nearly so comfortable here. They browsed, but they were obviously wary of being scammed. They haggled in many different languages but never in the native tongue. The vendors just did their business and tried to get as many bills off the people's piles as possible.

Jo poked around the little bits of Kinh-Sanhian junk—and junk from a dozen other countries. She found Chinese fans and handcuffs. Little Eiffel Towers. Austin Powers dolls. A vendor selling nothing but pirated American music on cassette. And clothes. Lots and lots of clothes.

Some of it wasn't too tacky, either.

Hmmm, maybe this country isn't such a nightmare after all, Jo thought. She browsed through a few racks, inspecting cuffs, hemlines, and collar styles with a trained eye.

Suddenly someone tapped her on the shoulder.

"Help you, pretty miss?" a wizened old Kinh-Sanh man asked. "Twenty dollar."

Jo grinned wide, immediately slipping into superflirt mode. She spoke with a slight Spanish accent. "Ah, hello. You speak English?"

The man nodded. "Little enough."

"Fantastic. I've been all over this city, and no one wants to help me," she pouted.

"I help," the vendor replied with a proud smile. "I get you supercool T-shirt. Twenty dollar."

Jo grinned. "I'll buy five T-shirts if you can help me."

The vendor's eyes lit up. "You make me very happy. I help!"

"Oh, thank you," Jo said, touching the man's arm. "I've come all the way from Madrid, and I'm totally lost. Do you know anything about a man named West? Lucien West?"

The vendor's expression turned to disgust. "Ugh! You mean stinkball Luscious."

Jo's heart jumped. "Yes, that's him. Luscious Lucien West. I've come to find him. I hear he's the superguru of Kinh-Sanh." Jo leaned in close and elbowed the angry vendor. "I hear Lucien West can sell inner peace to the Dalai Lama himself."

"Beh!" the vendor growled, spitting. "All he do is set up shop in our beautiful country. Steal money. Steal lives. He evil man. I not help." The man waved her away. "You go now."

Jo slowly sulked away, pretending to be disappointed.

Hmmm. *That* was interesting. Not everyone thought Lucien was the cat's nip.

She moved on through the crowd. She tried to space them out, putting on her little Spanish girl lost act for a few more vendors. The reactions were all the same. "He set up shop. He evil man." One supergenerous woman tried to convince Jo to come home with her rather than go to Lucien. Jo politely refused but bought a couple of the plastic key chains she was selling.

After a while Jo glanced at her watch. Wow! She'd spent three hours in the market. Well, she figured, that's nothing new. This was Kinh-Sanh's version of the mall, and three hours in a mall was just a warm-up for Jo. She was about to head back to the flat when she spotted something familiar.

A flash of color.

Silk blouses on a rack. The exact same pattern as the sleeve scrap they found in the warehouse!

Jo hurried over and snagged one off the rack. It was nice enough, but the print wasn't her at all. She checked the label—and her jaw dropped. The label said Girl Talk!

And it was in capital letters. It was a knockoff of Theresa's mother's design!

Well, the fact that it was a cheap copy explained the obnoxious print. But how would a rackful of bogus Girl Talks find their way into a seedy market when they should be hanging out at Bogart's fifth floor?

Jo immediately bought one of every color for about ten U.S. dollars each.

As she hightailed it back to the flat, she couldn't help but grin. She had just combined the thrill of shopping, the excitement of finding an extreme bargain, and the rush of saving the world all at once!

Did she have the life or *what?*

The noonday sun beamed happily down on the garden near the main temple. Caylin sat with Jenny and a half dozen other members she had just met. Her indoctrination had begun in earnest, and the members sat in the warm sun reminiscing about their first days in the compound. The one common thread Caylin found between all of them?

Too much money.

But Lucien was doing his best to help cure them of it.

"I feel so free," a girl named Concetta said, holding her arms out to soak in the sunbeams. "Everything I used to worry about means nothing. It is true freedom, Caylin. You'll know what we mean very soon."

Concetta came from Milan. From what she had said before, her father owned a vineyard that produced some of the finest wine in northern Italy. Big bucks. But for some reason, wine barrels full of cash weren't enough to fulfill Concetta's sense of self-worth.

"Listen to her, Caylin," Barry from London advised. "She was one of the most lost causes you ever saw when she came in here. But look at her now. A veritable font of tranquility."

The others laughed. Barry came from a distinguished British publishing family. He fled Cambridge for a chain-smoking trip across Asia. Then he found Lucien, smoked his last butt, and never left. He didn't even miss the nicotine.

"Inner peace can be catching," added Stanislaus from Prague.

There were others: Molly from Seattle (her father was a computer game designer); Ito from Nagasaki (his father was into Japanese steel and golf course development); Gunther from Zurich (banking); Heddy from Iceland (designer soft drinks); Louis from Jamaica (resort development and agriculture).

What was amazing to Caylin was that there were over sixty others who she hadn't met yet. What did *their* parents do? Best-selling authors? Tax lawyers? Senators? It boggled the mind.

She'd learned more about Jenny, too. Her mother was a real estate developer in the Chicago suburbs. Jenny had begun college but quickly fell into the wrong crowd. Drinking. Partying. Learning very little except how to skip class. Eventually Jenny scammed a hunk of money from one of her tuition accounts and headed out. By the time she got to Lucien, the rest of her tuition money was safely in her bag, in cash, waiting for the proper moment to be spent.

That moment came on Jenny's second day at

the compound. Since then she was able to get Lucien some other account numbers belonging to her mother. Jenny justified this by swearing that her mother had more than she could ever need. She said it with such shocking disgust that Caylin had to wonder what her mother ever did to deserve it.

"So what does your father do?" Ito asked her.

Caylin shrugged. "He's an oil rancher. So was my grandfather and my great-grandfather."

"There's oil in Nebraska?" Molly from Seattle asked skeptically.

"No," Caylin replied. "In Texas. We just live in Nebraska."

"I hope you realize how important it is for us to help Lucien any way we can," Jenny told her. "We were all unlucky to be born into unbelievable materialistic situations. Luckily we don't have to live with it."

"It's also lucky that most of us are able to siphon some of that wealth to Lucien," Barry said. "I don't know what I would do if this place ever shut down. I'd have no place to go."

Caylin smiled and nodded in agreement. But inside, she just couldn't believe it. Were their lives so bad? So empty? Actually, they sounded too *full*. The way she saw it, they were just a bunch of spoiled rich kids who suddenly realized that they were at an age when people expected them to take responsibility for their lives. Get the expensive degrees. Take over the family businesses. Make something of themselves.

Grow up.

None of them wanted to do that. They had taken their deep-seated aversion to real life and used it as a springboard to brainwashing. Lucien was a dream of an authority figure—he put no pressure on them as long as the cash rolled in. It was as if they were paying him to protect them from the real world.

Ha. Not a bad setup.

But Caylin also realized that she was being harsh. She doubted that any of their decisions had been conscious. They looked ahead at their responsibilities and couldn't handle what they saw. Instinctively they rebelled. Fled to a place where the pastures were greener than any they had ever seen. Greener than cold, hard cash at any rate.

Yet down to the last one she had met, they seemed happy. Their "inner peace" was genuine. Inside these walls, stress was extinct.

Caylin couldn't really fault them for wanting true inner peace.

A bell rang from the temple. The group slowly got to their feet.

"What's that?" Caylin asked.

"The midday gathering," Jenny said, offering a hand to help her up. "Come on."

The group made their way toward the front of the temple. Small crowds of other members came out of buildings and copses of trees and other gardens. It was like a slow, serene stampede of white cloth.

Lucien calls, Caylin mused, and they come running.

She purposely lagged back from the group to watch them all more closely. But something distracted her.

A pair of sparkly white Range Rovers entered the compound and drove toward them. Their arrival was rather shocking since Caylin hadn't seen any hint of outside technology within the compound (other than Lucien's computer room). The SUVs' windows were tinted black. As they passed, Caylin tried to see inside. But no dice.

The Rovers proceeded to the back of the main temple, disappearing around the corner.

Hmmm.

Caylin glanced around. The rest of the group was intent on getting to the gathering. No one paid any attention to her.

Perfect.

She edged through some shrubbery to the side of the building and peered around the corner to check it out. The Range Rovers were backing up to a pair of steel double doors. When the SVUs stopped, the drivers—both burly shaved heads—dismounted and went straight for the doors. One knocked while the other opened the hatchbacks of the Rovers. Something wasn't right with these guys. What was it—?

Caylin stiffened.

They wore the regular "spiritual" garb like all the others. But in her spy training Caylin had seen enough concealed weapons to know that these two peace lovers were packing heat. The bulges were unmistakable.

What would cult members need with guns?

The double doors swung wide, and several more shaved heads carried out a bunch of large duffel bags. Judging by the effort, Caylin guessed the bags were full of something heavy. The guards tossed them into the back of the Range Rovers without a word.

In seconds the transaction was complete. The hatchbacks were slammed shut, the double doors closed, and the armed drivers got back in and put the SVUs in gear.

This was huge. She wasn't exactly sure what she'd seen, but weapons and bags and secret exchanges sure *felt* huge. Caylin had to get to her phone. She'd stashed it in her room, frustrated like crazy because she didn't have anywhere to carry it. But this definitely deserved a phone call to the other Spy Girls.

"Hey!" a voice called from behind her.

Caylin froze, fear streaking down her spine.

Somehow a phone call didn't seem to be in her future.

Caylin whirled.

Jenny!

"What are you doing?" she demanded.

Caylin grinned. "Just looking around. I'm still kind of lost around here."

Jenny shook her head. "All you had to do was follow us. Come on, we'll miss the gathering!"

Caylin nodded and went with her, reminding herself to let out a really heavy sigh of relief later. That was close!

She had to be more careful. The new person would arouse the most suspicion if she were continuously caught poking her nose around corners.

The only problem was that there always seemed to be something suspicious going on around those pesky corners.

But, Caylin thought desperately, what did it all mean?

"Eureka!" Theresa shouted.

Jo bolted into the flat's computer room,

93

wondering who won the lottery. There was Theresa, hair shooting up in all directions, bags under her bloodshot eyes, arms raised in victory. Her ridiculous grin made her look insane.

"What?" Jo asked.

"I did it!" She held up a sheaf of laser printouts. "I hacked that sucker wide open! Just call me Madam Machete!"

"If you don't get a grip, I'm going to start calling you Darla Demento," Jo said.

"Jo, do you realize what I've just gone through?" Theresa said, her eyes wild. "The security? The dead ends? The mazes? I've just done an iron woman triathalon of a hack! And I got a ton!"

"A ton of what?" Jo asked, wrinkling her nose.

Theresa wiggled her eyebrows. "Numbers, my dear. Lots and lots of numbers. Take a look."

Theresa scrolled down a screen filled with numerical entries. Figures flew by in a blizzard.

"Slow down!" Jo ordered. "What is all this?"

"It's one of Lucien's financial ledgers," Theresa explained, brandishing a crumpled printout. "This is what we've been looking for."

"That's great, but what's in it?" Jo repeated.

"Millions." Theresa clicked the mouse as the numbers continued to fly. "He's got millions of dollars passing back and forth to various accounts. They all seem to start out as this vague description called 'donations.' But that doesn't make any sense at all."

"Why not?" Jo asked. "He's running a spiritual retreat, after all."

Theresa shook her head. "We're talking nine figures here, Jo. Even if all the rich kids in the Western Hemisphere got together and pooled their trust funds, they'd never be able to slap together this kind of money. And they're all 'cash' transactions that are basically untraceable."

"So he is into something crooked," Jo declared.

"Well, his books are crooked, that's for sure," Theresa said, leaning back in her chair. "Just from an accounting standpoint, he's a first-rate con artist. But the real question is, where does the money come from?"

"Drugs?" Jo speculated, squinting at the screen.

Theresa shook her head doubtfully. "I think Uncle Sam would've known about that. No, this is something different. But what?"

"Have you saved all this stuff?" Jo asked.

"Are you kidding? I downloaded it as soon as I found it. I wasn't going to let this guy get the best of—"

Theresa's eyes bugged at her screen.

"Oh no, not again!"

She typed frantically, then dove across the desk and yanked the cords out of the back of her little black box. The system shut down with an electronic thunk.

"They nuke you again?" Jo asked.

Theresa stood, frozen. "No. That was something different. Someone was tracking my hack. Not just back to my computer, but to our actual address."

"Did you get out in time?" Jo asked nervously.

"I think so," Theresa said, looking at the black box as if the bad guys were going to pop out of it.

"You *think* so?" Jo screeched. "If a bunch of bald bikers pull up outside, I'm handing you over."

Theresa laughed. "Don't worry, Jo. I got out."

Jo slumped against the wall. "So what do we do now?"

"We can show all this data to Sammy. He might have a suggestion. Or . . ."

"Or what?" Jo prompted.

"Well . . . there was something else in that ledger," Theresa said, rubbing her weary eyes. "But I have no idea what it means. Something called 'the Purchase.'"

Jo shrugged. "What is it?"

"Earth to Jo," Theresa said, waving a hand in front of Jo's eyes. "I just said I don't know. But think about it. What do you buy with that much money?"

"The Yankees," Jo replied.

"I doubt it," Theresa said. "But I bet all that cash would go a lot further in a third world country like Kinh-Sanh than it would in the United States. A *lot* further."

"That makes sense," Jo agreed. "But other than that, what do we really have?"

Theresa smiled lamely. "Nothing."

"Right. Which either means you're going to have to do some more creative hacking, or we're going to have to find an alternate means of fact-finding," Jo said.

Theresa deflated and plopped back into her chair. "I'm done with the laptop for a while. Even if I could keep my eyes open, Lucien's computer squad is looking for me now. I wouldn't get anywhere."

"I thought so," Jo said with a nod. "That's why I took it upon myself to hit the streets while your nose was pressed up against your screen."

She tossed a rumpled garment into Theresa's lap.

"What's this?" Theresa asked.

Jo grinned. "I don't know if it has anything to do with anything, but check out the print."

Theresa's eyes widened in recognition. "It's the same silk pattern we found in the warehouse!"

"Correct-amundo," Jo said, leaning against the desk. "Now check out the label."

Theresa's eyes grew even wider. "My mom's label! It's a total rip-off!"

"Two for two," Jo said, holding up her hands in two peace signs. "Aren't you glad you told that stupid story about the capital letters to us?"

"It's not stupid." Theresa scowled. "It's a very fond memory of my childhood."

"Then you had a lame childhood," Jo teased. "The point is, I wouldn't have recognized it otherwise. But don't you think it's a little strange that the same pattern that is on the floor in Lucien's warehouse is available for ten bucks in the market district?"

Theresa blinked. "You paid ten bucks for this? Even the knockoffs are fifty in the States."

"Can I sniff the bargains or what?" Jo said triumphantly.

Theresa smirked. "You're going to wear this?"

"Are you nuts?" Jo blurted out. "I wouldn't wear that to your funeral. I wouldn't wear that to Mike Schaeffer's funeral!"

"Who's Mike Schaeffer?" Theresa asked, her brow furrowing.

Jo scowled. "Nobody."

"Jooooooo . . . ," Theresa sang.

"He's nobody. Just an old—no, make that an *ancient* flame. He's the reason the word *jerk* is so deeply tattooed on my brain."

Theresa's grin widened. "So . . . a little chunk of the past life breaks loose. Was he cute?"

Jo growled impatiently. "We're not talking about this now. End of story. *Finito*. Sign off, Little Miss Modem."

"Well, pardon me all over town," Theresa said, grinning up at Jo. "All I asked was if you'd wear my mother's designs."

Jo held up one of the obnoxious knockoffs. "Your mother didn't design this! She'd keel over if she saw it. This is what frat boys wear to their spring flings."

She tossed it over her shoulder in disgust.

"But Jo," Theresa said playfully. "You bought *six* of them. Why did you buy so many if you weren't going to wear them? One would've been plenty if you were just going to show me the bogus label."

"I was *not* going to wear them," Jo said in a threatening voice. "I stand by my previous statements regarding funerals. Which is what you'll be attending if you don't lay off."

"Oh yeah, the Mike Schaeffer affair," Theresa replied. "Who was he again?"

"Auuuuuggggggghhhhh!" Jo bellowed. She scooped up the other obnoxious shirts and hurled them at Theresa. T. giggled and slipped out of her chair to the floor. Shirts hung off her as if she were a brightly dressed scarecrow.

After a few seconds of staring, all the two of them could do was sit there and laugh.

Finally Jo slumped to the floor with Theresa. "Before you took me on that charming trip down bad-memory lane, I did have a point."

"I see," Theresa replied. "And what might that point be?"

"I think a return trip to the warehouse is in order," she suggested. "But we'll be a little more professional this time. We go under cover of night. With the proper gear. And the proper attire."

"You mean the shirts?" Theresa asked.

"I mean proper evening wear," Jo said, a sly grin appearing on her face. *"All black."*

It was nearly midnight when they were ready.

Jo emerged from her room clad in a black turtleneck and tight black jeans. She clicked on a leather fanny pack that held a few basics: pepper spray perfume, compact communicator, mascara dart gun with sleep-tipped darts. You know, the essentials.

She caught a look at herself in the mirror. "Oo, baby, you are just too hot to handle." She smooched at her reflection.

"You're gonna make me puke," Theresa muttered. She had opted for a black sweater and loose-fitting black jeans rather than the skintight outerwear.

"I'd love a black leather cat suit," Jo remarked, inspecting her profile. She ran a hand over her stomach. "Sort of an Emma Peel thing."

"The sailors down on the wharf would love it," Theresa said. She tucked a minicamera and her glasses into a zipper pouch in the sweater. "But that *is* your crowd."

Jo applied some lipstick and puckered her lips to even it out. "I am unappreciated in my own time. Are we ready to go yet?"

"I've been ready for ten minutes," Theresa complained. "The bad guys could've taken over the Alamo by now, and you're primping."

"I refuse to go into battle with a shiny nose," Jo declared, applying powder.

"You're gonna go with a bloody nose if you don't—"

A loud beeping cut Theresa off. What was that? The phone. But who would be calling at this hour?

Jo and Theresa realized it simultaneously: "Caylin!"

They dove for the phone and snapped it up, holding it between their ears.

"Hello!" they said in unison.

"Hey, guys," came Caylin's hushed voice. "It's me."

"Where are you?" Jo asked.

"I'm in a shower stall. Everyone's asleep. I figured I should check in. It's been . . . interesting."

"What happened?" Theresa asked, whispering, too.

Caylin quickly ran down her string of events, from meeting Lucien to seeing the computers to the men with guns and duffels.

"Yeah, well, those computer geeks are probably in it up to here," Theresa said proudly. "I broke in tonight. And we got an eyeful."

She and Jo shared their side of the story, down to the last brush burn from the cycle chase.

"So what do you think 'the Purchase' is?" Jo asked.

"Your guess is as good as mine," Caylin replied. "The only thing Lucien talked about was a recreation facility downtown and a new retreat. Oh yeah, and franchises."

"Franchises?" Jo asked. "Sheesh."

Theresa frowned and shook her head. "That's small fries compared to the amounts of money we're talking about. This is going to be big, whatever it is."

"I don't know," Caylin said. "*Something* is going on. We just have to dig deeper."

"Actually, we were just about to do that," Jo replied. "We're hitting the warehouse again tonight."

"That's probably a good idea," Caylin said. "Be careful. There might be something worse than killer bikers this time."

"Will do," Theresa said. Then she smiled. "It's good to hear your voice. How are they treating you?"

Caylin laughed. "The place really is paradise, if you're into that kind of thing. I prefer something a little more down-to-earth mys—"

Suddenly Caylin's voice was cut off.

"Cay?" Jo called.

No answer. Something came across from the background. A gruff voice.

"Caylin, are you there?" Theresa asked.

There was a thunk. Some static.

Then the line went dead.

Caylin huddled in the cramped shower stall, smelling the mildew, gripping her tiny cell phone, and staring up at Jenny.

"What are you doing?" Jenny demanded, scowling. "That's an unauthorized phone. That should be in storage with the rest of your personal belongings. And you know the rules: No outside contact until your indoctrination period is over!"

Caylin slumped down farther. "I know, but . . ."

"But what?" Jenny scolded, obviously trying not to raise her voice. "If any of the others wake up and find us in here, we could both be excommunicated! I worked too hard, and I'm not going to get thrown out because of you."

Easy, girl, Caylin thought angrily. This isn't NASA. The only hard work it took for you to get through the gate was carrying a bag of cash and memorizing a Swiss account number.

Caylin stopped herself. She was undercover. But Jenny was really here, in every sense of the word. This was her world, no matter how Caylin felt about that.

"I'm sorry," Caylin whispered, her shoulders sagging.

"Who are you talking to?" Jenny demanded.

Caylin fidgeted. "My, um . . . my boyfriend."

Jenny rolled her eyes. "I should've known. If it's not parents, then it's boyfriends. Well, we haven't lost anyone yet to a boyfriend, and I'm not about to start now. Come out of there."

"I'm sorry, Jenny," Caylin said lamely. "He's in Berlin, and I just miss him so much. My parents were a nightmare, but he was the only person I could really talk to."

Jenny nodded and offered her hand. "They always are. Come on."

Caylin took her hand and stood, not quite sure how to take Jenny's reaction. So far, this seemed like a pretty normal thing. Even kids who hate their homes can get homesick.

"What's his name?" Jenny asked, hands on hips.

Caylin thought quickly. "Sam."

"What's he doing in Berlin?"

Caylin smiled awkwardly and shrugged. "The same thing I'm doing in the Orient. Wandering around. He likes Europe too much to wander anywhere else."

"How much did you tell him about this place?" Jenny asked, her tone very serious.

"Nothing," Caylin replied, shivering. The cold and dampness of the shower room was taking its toll on her. "If he knew I'd joined up with something like this, he'd go nuts. He'd probably even tell my parents. As far as he knows, I'm just wandering from place to place."

Jenny thought about her answer for a moment and apparently decided to accept it because she didn't ask anything else. Then she put out her hand.

"Give me the phone," Jenny ordered.

She sounds like Miss Buszko in kindergarten, Caylin thought. Sheesh.

"Aw, Jenny," Caylin whined. "Just let me keep it, huh? I promise I won't use it."

"Then what's the point of keeping it?" Jenny challenged.

Caylin deflated. "Come on. . . ."

"Caylin, if you're going to stay here, you have to abide by the rules. Even the ones you don't agree with. That's part of the sacrifice we all make."

"I'm trying, Jenny," Caylin replied. "Really."

"I know," Jenny said, nodding. "But to find true inner peace, you must forget about the outside world. Even Sam in Berlin. He can't help you from thousands of miles away. When you have a problem or feel weak, come talk to me. I've been through it all, trust me." Just when Caylin thought Jenny was softening, the glorious mentor held out her hand again. "But you have to start by giving up the phone. Right now."

Caylin wasn't worried about losing the phone. She was worried about giving it up to Jenny. It was a Tower communications device, with all the bells and whistles. If Jenny decided to play with it, she might hit the wrong button and ring Uncle Sam's vacation home in Monte Carlo. Or worse.

She simply couldn't give Jenny that phone.

"I'll tell you what. I'll go you one better," Caylin offered.

She set the tiny phone down on the tile floor. Then she stomped on it with all her might. The plastic gave a loud crunch. The soft white shoes didn't give much padding, and a bolt of pain shot up Caylin's leg. But she'd felt worse and didn't flinch.

The phone was toast.

Caylin smiled. "That way no one is tempted. Right?"

Jenny returned the smile. "Maybe you'll fit in here after all. Come on. You need your rest. Tomorrow's a big day."

Caylin nodded and followed. But the blissful smile on her face was false as a cosmetic eyelash. The lump in her throat was real. For now she had absolutely no way of contacting the Spy Girls!

*　　*　　*

"What do we do?" Jo asked, fear gripping her heart. "Caylin could be busted!"

"There's nothing we can do, Jo." Theresa shook her head. "And you know it. Cay's on her own. If she blows her cover, then she has to handle it. Our mission parameters are clear. Read your manual."

"You know what you can do with your manual, O Goddess of the Geeks," Jo said, eyes flashing. "We're talking about Caylin here!"

Theresa frowned. "I know. Don't think for a second that I don't. But you know there is nothing we can do. We don't know if she was busted or not."

Jo slumped down into the mountain of pillows. She sighed in futility. "I know. But it makes me crazy sometimes."

"Me too. But all we can do is head to the warehouse as scheduled. If she can, she'll make contact with us soon enough."

Jo looked up at Theresa with worried eyes. "And if she can't?"

Theresa smiled lamely. "I didn't hear that, Jo. Let's roll."

The night air was chilly, but Theresa and Jo were dressed for it: scalp-to-toe black. Even T. had to admit that they looked pretty hot—true superspies if there ever were any. As they passed from the thin late-night crowds of the tourist district to the deserted alleys of the waterfront, no one paid them any mind. Just two more wandering souls trying to find the best place to hole up for the night, right?

They passed by the site where the truck ran over their motorcycle. The whole mess had been cleaned up. Not a speck of broken glass remained.

"Wow," Theresa marveled. "In my hometown they can't even fix potholes."

"It's pretty amazing when a city keeps the streets clean even in the neighborhoods that smell like dead fish," Jo agreed.

They arrived at the warehouse just before 1 A.M.

Theresa paused. "Someone's been here."

"How do you know?" Jo asked.

"Check it out." A shiny new padlock hung from the main door.

"Should we burn it off again?" Jo asked.

Theresa shook her head. "They might be watching. Or waiting inside. Let's go around the other side and see if there's another way in."

They crept around to the side facing the docks. A massive cargo ship was moored a few hundred feet down the pier. And a large panel truck was backed up against the warehouse's loading platform. One of the garage doors was open.

Uh-oh, Theresa thought. Someone's home.

Suddenly a lighter flickered in the darkness.

Jo and Theresa flattened themselves against the wall of the warehouse.

Theresa made out the silhouette of a large, bald man. He lit a cigarette and puffed away. He didn't see them.

Theresa fished out a tiny pair of binoculars and flipped them open. They were equipped with green night vision, which allowed her to see just about everything in the dark.

"I still think you get the coolest gear," Jo whispered.

"If you'd show up at your surveillance training classes, they might actually trust you with some of this stuff," Theresa replied.

"Yeah, yeah, yeah, Lucy Lecture," Jo muttered. "What do you see?"

Theresa squinted through the lens, her heart pounding. "Three guys. They're unloading something from the truck into the warehouse."

"Are they duffel bags?" Jo asked, remembering what Caylin had seen.

"No," Theresa said, trying to focus better. It didn't help that her hands were shaking. She forced herself to concentrate. "These look like heavy-duty suitcases. Metal. There's some writing on the side. I can't really make it out. It's not English, though."

"Asian lettering?"

Theresa shook her head. "Maybe Russian."

One of the men on the loading dock tripped. His suitcase clanked to the ground, and he went flying. The big man tossed his cigarette aside angrily and let out a string of curses in some foreign language. At least, it sounded foreign. And they sounded like curses.

The clumsy man stood up, grabbed the big suitcase, and continued on his way.

"They're all going inside," Theresa said, following them with her night vision.

"Let's go," Jo replied, tugging T.'s sleeve.

Theresa yanked loose. "Okay, okay. But *quietly*."

"No duh," Jo grumbled.

"They have guns, Jo," Theresa warned. "Aren't you the least bit nervous?"

Jo grinned in the moonlight. "*Nervous* is not in my vocabulary."

"I'll take that as a big yes," Theresa muttered. "Come on."

They slipped onto the loading dock and cautiously peeked inside the truck. It was empty.

Whatever they're delivering is inside already, Theresa thought. Which means we have to go inside, too. Great.

Theresa made fists to keep her hands from trembling. She jerked her head toward the door, motioning for Jo to go. Slowly the girls tiptoed into the warehouse. Both of them wore special soft-soled, Tower-issued shoes that masked most sound. But even they couldn't prevent the occasional creaking of the ancient warehouse floor—which sent rivers of ice up Theresa's spine every time.

"Shhh," Jo warned.

"We should've brought wings and flown in," Theresa remarked.

They waited until the last man disappeared around a corner, then advanced. The men paid no attention to anything around them, shooting comments back and forth and laughing occasionally. When the big cigarette guy cursed at them again, they shut up.

The men eventually stopped in front of a wall on the main floor of the empty warehouse. Theresa noticed that it wasn't far from where they had picked up the silk sleeve. Two more men waited for them. Five in all. With three suitcases.

What are they doing? Theresa wondered, her pulse pounding in her ears. And what's in the Samsonite?

The big man stepped forward and clicked something on the wall—and a whole section swung inward!

"Secret door," Jo whispered, grabbing Theresa's arm like a vise. "*That's* why we couldn't find a basement. It's hidden."

Theresa nodded excitedly. They crept closer, pausing behind a pile of splintered wood next to a cement pillar. Theresa felt the grit grinding beneath her feet, but the special shoes kept it silent. Thank God.

The men bobbed and sank into the floor as they went through the door—as if they were going down a flight of steps. Finally the last man slipped through the door, and it swung shut with a clunk.

The girls hurried over to it.

"Give them a second to move on," Theresa warned, holding Jo's arm. "We don't want to run up their backs."

"We still don't know where the switch is," Jo reminded her, running her fingers along the smooth wall. Bits of soot fell through her fingers to the floor. She found nothing.

"It has to be here somewhere," Theresa said, picking at every little imperfection in the paint. She probed the specific section of wall that she saw the man touch. "The big guy touched right here. Or close to here."

"Better hurry, or we'll lose them," Jo said.

"Yeah, they might take those steps all the way down to China," Theresa replied. "Or Toledo. Or whatever's currently on the opposite side of the planet."

"You're not nice," Jo quipped.

"Aw, you just don't know me," Theresa answered.

Adrenaline shot through her veins when her fingers brushed over a small imperfection in the wall. She frantically dug in her fingernails and pulled down a small lever made of the same plaster as the wall.

"Got it!" she said triumphantly, instantly regretting how loud she was.

But it was too late for that—the wall swung inward.

Beyond was a pitch black staircase. All Theresa could see were a few steps leading down. Then nothing. The men ahead must have moved on—there wasn't a sound to be heard.

Theresa peeked through her night vision binocs.

"It's blurry because we're so close," she whispered. "But the stairs go down."

Jo rolled her eyes. "I'm blind, and I can see that. How far?"

"About twenty feet. I can't tell for sure, but it looks like a dead end."

They started down. The steps and walls were made of interlocking stone. It smelled damp and ancient. They ran their hands along the side for support.

"I don't hear them," Theresa said, bumping Jo's shoulder.

"All I hear is you," Jo replied, shoving her back.

"Watch it, Spy Girl," T. warned. "It's a long way down."

Jo chuckled nervously. "How do you know that?"

"Gut feeling," Theresa said with a shrug no one could see.

Finally they reached the bottom. There was a square yard's worth of landing, but no way out. They were surrounded by stone walls.

"There has to be another secret door," Theresa said.

"You think?" Jo joked.

They searched, but in the dark all they could do was feel. Crumbs of old mortar fell away from the joints. They did everything—they pulled, they pushed, they felt for something other than stone. Jo even checked for a good old doorknob. But nothing.

"You know what would be a cool gadget?" Jo asked.

"What?" Theresa replied, feeling along the top of the wall.

"A secret door detector."

Theresa chuckled. "Good point. Make a note of it."

"T., we checked every inch of these walls," Jo said, crossing her arms across her chest. "It's just not here."

"It has to be," Theresa grumbled. "Five steroid thugs with Russian Samsonites can't just evaporate. We have to check again. We must have missed—"

Theresa paused.

"What?" Jo asked.

"We didn't check the floor."

"Grrr," Jo growled. She sank to her knees. "Now I'm reduced to feeling around on my hands and knees?"

"No, no, stand up," Theresa told her. "It's probably just a little pressure plate. Something quick and simple that you could find in the dark."

She began tapping every little stone she could feel.

"Hey—I have a loose one over here!" Jo said excitedly. She hopped up and down on it, but nothing happened. "No fair."

"Keep hopping. It just might be—"

Theresa's toe tapped a stone, and she heard a click.

The wall to their left popped outward several inches. A crack of light seeped through.

"That's it!" Theresa said. "Open sesame seed buns."

"What do you mean 'that's it'? My rock opened the door."

"No way," Theresa argued. "I felt a distinct click when I stepped on this rock right here."

She tapped her toe for emphasis.

"I don't hear any click," Jo said.

Theresa rolled her eyes. "The door's not going to click when it's *open*, brain cell. Can we move on, please?"

"Glory hog." Jo shoved past her and slowly pushed on the open door.

"Return to stealth mode," Theresa whispered.

The stone door swung easily on greased hinges. The light ahead was dim, but sunlike compared to the dungeon they just came from.

The secret door clicked shut behind them.

When their eyes adjusted, they found themselves on a rusty steel balcony at the top of a long metal staircase, like a fire escape. But they weren't on the side of a building—they were deep inside the subbasement of the warehouse. The floor was two stories below. So far down that it might as well have been two miles.

Jo and Theresa stared at the scene below, mouths gaping.

"Oh my gosh . . . ," Theresa whispered.

Twenty feet below Jo and Theresa lay a massive chamber full of Kinh-Sanhians. Two hundred. Maybe three. And each was chained to a grimy sewing machine. Men, women, children even—they all hunched over their machines, churning out piece after piece of flashy clothing. Grime coated the workers. The scraps they wore looked like they were made from unusable bits of the cloth they worked on.

Armed guards—all of them with shaved heads—walked among the rows of machines. They barked occasional orders but mostly just hung back, made jokes, and smoked cigarettes.

The place sounded like a demented barnyard. One machine ran for a few seconds, then another one across the room answered it. The air smelled like stale cigarette smoke, machine oil, and sweat. Bad sweat. The kind of sweat that was tinged with fear.

"Look at them all," Jo whispered. "They're like zombies."

Her eyes fell on one worker in particular, a skin-and-bones child who mindlessly fed cloth into her machine. A combination of anger and pity rose in Jo. Her mouth filled with the taste of copper. The taste of pure adrenaline.

"Underfed zombies," Theresa replied angrily. "This is a sweatshop, Jo. A real, live sweatshop."

"So that's Lucien's secret," Jo reasoned. "But those people . . . they look like they're right off the street."

"They probably are," Theresa replied. "Think about it. The city streets seemed so nice and clean. Especially in the tourist district. I bet Lucien and his thugs kidnap homeless people and throw them down here to make his designer knockoffs."

"And he pockets the cash," Jo finished.

"Exactly." Theresa scowled. "Courtesy of my mother's good name and label. This guy makes me want to barf. He deserves to die for what he's doing to these people."

"T, how PG-13 of you," Jo replied. "I think we'll just have to settle with destroying his operation, unmasking him as a sham, and sending him to prison for the rest of his life."

"That's like winning the lame half of *The Price Is Right* showcase. But it'll have to do." Theresa rubbed her chin. "Still, something doesn't add up."

"What's that?"

"Let's get out of here and I'll tell you. We're sitting ducks up here." Theresa turned to the secret door, but it was just a blank wall. "Oh no."

Panic gripped Jo as the two of them ran their hands over the rough surface, trying to slip into the cracks where the door met the wall.

It was no use.

There was no latch on this side.

They were trapped!

Finishing her Tower training was easy. The triathlon in Greece, that was easy, too. And Caylin's final test for her black belt? The moves were so natural to her that that had been the easiest challenge of all.

So was slipping out of the dorm. All she'd needed was a little speed, a little stealth maneuvering, and the ability to hide around corners as baldies patrolled the hallways.

Now came the hard part.

Caylin couldn't get an exact time (they took her watch), but it had to be around one or two in the morning. Everyone was asleep. From what she could see, there were no guards roaming the compound.

But there were plenty of cameras.

She had spent most of the afternoon in the compound with Jenny and her cronies. Plenty of time to note the location of each camera. And how long it took to make its mechanical sweep.

Now all she had to do was run it like an obstacle course. She would wait for the camera to turn away, then dart to the next bit of cover.

Simple, right?

Caylin hoped so.

She fixed on the first camera, and after a moment sprinted across the grass to a pair of trees. There she waited.

She wished she had something other than her bright whites to wear. But maybe that was the point. They were easy for the baldies to spot. There was never any question who wore them. Oh, well, it wasn't like she had a choice.

Caylin had grown quite sick of sitting around in her room. No books. No music. No gym. It was prison for her—and she'd only been there for twenty-four hours! She tried to imagine what it would be like to actually *live* there. Breakdown time!

Now that she had lost her phone, she figured it was time to get a little more aggressive. She had to do some serious snooping. She'd never find anything out during the light of day. There were too many peace-and-love activities, and she'd had more than enough of that.

The next camera turned away.

Caylin bolted, covering the distance to the next group of trees in seconds.

The next camera was high above her, attached to the main temple. That would be the tricky one—it didn't move. It was aimed along the side of the building, toward the rear. Which was exactly where Caylin was going. She would have to take the chance that no one was looking at that monitor at that moment. Because she really didn't have an excuse if she got caught this time.

No boyfriend. No searching for the bathroom. No taking a midnight stroll. She'd be as busted as busted can be.

Oh, well, better busted than bored, she figured.

She took a deep breath. Willed whoever was watching to look away.

And she ran.

The moon cast a long shadow on that side of the temple, helping her hide. Would it be enough? It had to be.

Her legs pumped hard. The grass passed beneath her, and her hair whipped back from her face. She felt like she was going a hundred miles an hour. But she was still so slow, so slow.

They had to see her.

A guard dozing on a bench. The security guy checking the cameras. Lucien gazing out his beautiful windows. Someone.

Finally Caylin reached the spot where she'd seen the Range Rovers that day. She slipped around the corner of the temple and plastered herself against the wall. Her breathing was controlled, steady. The adrenaline was exhilarating.

Now *this* is what I call inner peace! she thought.

She held her breath for a few seconds, listening.

Nothing.

Looks like I pulled it off. For now . . .

She padded across the gravel to the steel double doors at the back of the temple and pulled on the large handle. Locked, naturally.

Caylin reached up and produced the last piece of hardware she had. The only thing she could hide from Jenny and the vulture who took all her stuff—a bobby pin.

She hoped she could do it. Jo had done it once, in a wine cellar in Prague, of all places. Over time, it became a kind of competition between the Spy Girls. Jo was the master. Even Theresa could do it if her life depended on it.

But Caylin had never been able to pull it off.

Now it counted. Now it was for real.

"Here goes nothing," she whispered.

Caylin bent the pin like she was supposed to. She slid it into the lock. Jiggled it. Pushed it.

Jiggled it. Tried to turn it but couldn't. She jiggled it some more.

Something clicked.

A wave of hope swept through her. She tried to turn the pin like a key.

It didn't budge.

Caylin sighed. Wiped her hands on her pants. Told herself to take her time, even though she knew that was the one thing she *couldn't* do. How long until a guard strolled by?

She jiggled it again. Wiggled, jiggled, squiggled—nothing worked.

Finally she took a deep breath. Held it. Closed her eyes. And slid the pin into the lock again. Gave it a gentle tug. Then twisted.

The pin turned!

The lock clicked aside, and the door opened!

Caylin beamed in triumph. Wait until the others heard about that! Picked a lock on a field mission! She was a true spy now!

She slipped through the door and quietly closed it behind her, then slid the lucky bobby pin back into her hair, vowing never to go anywhere without it.

Caylin took a quick look around. She was in a brick hallway. A short flight of concrete stairs ran down in front of her. Fluorescent lights were mounted in the walls every ten feet. Very plain, compared to the Taj upstairs.

Caylin snuck down the stairs and made her way along a corridor. Turned right. Turned left. She passed a series of doorways. The chambers were mostly empty and dim, save for some tables and folding chairs. The air smelled like a bad frat house cigar.

She paused before one doorway. A light shone out into the hall. Someone hummed inside.

Uh-oh, Caylin thought nervously. We've made contact. Intelligent life exists in the basement.

Slowly, carefully, she dared a peek around the corner.

A shave head sat with his back to her, puffing a cigar. But he wasn't wearing his robes. He wore a tank top and boxer shorts with big red hearts on them. A bunch of empty beer cans were stacked in a pyramid in front of him. Well-worn playing cards covered the table—a half-finished game of solitaire. A rack of poker chips sat to his left. The song he hummed was "Mmmbop," of all things.

He was cleaning a nine-millimeter pistol with a soiled rag. Two full magazines were within reach.

Some holy man, Caylin thought. Just as she suspected. They packed heat. She hadn't exactly expected the valentine undies, though.

Caylin tiptoed across the doorway and moved on.

She took a left and headed down another corridor. Actually, Caylin had no idea where she was going. All she knew was that she was somewhere underneath the main temple. Getting lost didn't really worry her—this maze had to open up *somewhere*. Getting caught, however, did worry her.

That's the real trick, isn't it? she thought as her slippered feet slid along the tile floor.

This particular hallway dead-ended at a steel door. When Caylin put her ear to it and listened, she heard nothing. The metal of the knob was cold and smooth on her palm—and turned easily.

She opened the door and peeked in.

Pitch black.

She felt the wall inside and found a light switch. But she slipped in and shut the door before flipping it on.

Caylin turned, and when she did, her mouth dropped open.

Holy college tuition, Batman, she thought.

The room was full of cash. Large bills, small bills, stacked, piled, bagged, and more. The far wall was literally a wall of money. The bundles were held together by bank bands and rubber bands. The stacks in turn were held together by plastic wrap. These cash "cubes" were about a foot square. Caylin figured there had to be at least fifty of them against the far wall alone. That didn't include the unwrapped millions all around her. A table held a counting machine and an adding machine big enough for Donald Trump's accountant. And in the corner to her left?

A big box filled with brand-new duffel bags—not even out of the wrapper yet.

"Whoa," she whispered.

There was enough cash here to finance a three-week Spy Girl shopping spree across London, Paris, and Milan!

So that's what was in the duffel bags. These cash cubes. It looked like they could fit about three cubes per bag. Which meant that they threw twelve cubes of cash in the back of those Range Rovers that afternoon.

Where was it going? And where did it come from?

Caylin knew that there was no way that much pure American currency could come from the cult members, as rich as they were. The short stack she handed over to Lucien was a cool ten grand of Tower money, and that was just a drop in the bucket compared to what was here.

This was huge. She had to find a way to contact the Spy Girls. Somehow. There must be some kind of communication device in Lucien's penthouse. If she could con her way up there

again . . . Lucien seemed to take a shine to her. . . .
Maybe she could sneak a call—

Something pressed against the back of her
neck. The tiny hairs stood up around it.

Caylin gulped, knowing immediately what
the object was from her training.

A gun barrel.

"Hiya, toots," came a gruff, shaved-headed
voice.

Don't tell me." Jo moaned, trying to block out the wails of the sewing machines below them.

"Okay, I won't," Theresa promised, running her hand along the door. "But we're trapped."

"I told you not to tell me!" Jo hissed.

"Since when do I listen to you?" Theresa said. "We have to get off this platform before one of the guards sees us."

"Or someone else comes through the secret door," Jo added, scanning the sweatshop below for a miracle. "What are the options?"

"Only one, Jo, and you know it," Theresa said, all business. "You see that dark archway at the far end of the shop?"

Jo squinted through the smoky air. There it was—a dark doorway in the very far wall. Jo gulped. They would have to sneak the length of the entire place to get there. It might as well have been a hundred miles across whoopie cushions.

Great, Jo thought. Just great.

131

"Yeah, I see it," she replied glumly. "But I don't believe it. Not for a second."

"We can do it," Theresa assured her.

"No, we can't."

"Jo, take a listen," Theresa ordered, nudging her. "We don't have to be quiet. They'll never hear us with all this racket. All we have to do is sneak around those carts with the clothes piled high. Invincible, invulnerable, invisible, remember?"

"You forgot inconceivable," Jo said, her eyes wide.

"Well, I'm going for it," Theresa said, reclipping her hair at the back of her head in preparation. "If we stay up here, we're definitely busted. By my count, there's six guards. They're lazy and scummy, and the last thing they'll expect to see is a couple of hot little spies running through their sweatshop. Let's go. On three."

"I hate this," Jo said angrily, checking the laces on her shoes. "And by osmosis I have come to hate you."

"Hate me later, Jo," Theresa said with a reassuring smile. "When we're sipping Earl Gray back at the flat."

Jo rolled her eyes. "On three," she replied, resigned.

Theresa nodded. "Three."

Then she started down the stairs.

"Hey!" Jo exclaimed. "Where's one and two?"

She moved quickly after Theresa, heart pounding, trying desperately to keep below the level of the railing. She figured their black forms would blend with the rusty black steel of the stairwell. Well, she *hoped* they did.

Suddenly Jo stumbled. Her stomach lurched into her throat as the long flight of steps rushed up to her.

She clawed for the railing, but it was too late.

Her arms pinwheeled helplessly and she pitched forward!

Caylin took a long, deep breath as Luscious Lucien West entered the cash room with two more shaved heads. He was dressed in full robes and looked relaxed and refreshed. His hair was perfect.

Does the man sleep? Caylin wondered.

He took one look at the guard who had found Caylin—the soiled-tank-top-and-valentine-boxers guy. "Good work, Lou. Go get some clothes on, will you?"

"Sure ting, boss," Lou replied. "Too much beauty'll burn yer eyes, right?"

"You're a charming man, Lou," Lucien said, his eyes boring into Caylin.

"Tanks, boss." He left.

"Well, well, well." Lucien shook his head. "Beautiful Caylin. You have no idea how disappointed I am to find you here."

"You have no idea how happy I am to disappoint you," Caylin replied, relieved to finally drop the simpering student act.

"A sharp wit to go with your charm," he replied with a smile. "What a waste. I thought we were becoming good friends." He raised her chin with his finger and looked into her eyes. "*Very* good friends."

Caylin yanked her chin out of his grip. "Once again, happy to disappoint you, Lucien. Or should I call you Carruthers?"

Caylin caught a glimpse of alarm on Lucien's face. But that's all it was—a glimpse. He ignored her accusation. "I suppose it's useless to ask what exactly you are doing down here?"

Caylin shrugged. "I wanted my money back."

Lucien chuckled. "Did you really think you could sneak around here without getting caught? I mean, you seem like such a clever girl."

"Not clever enough, I guess," Caylin replied. "But at least I don't have a cellar full of stolen cash keeping me up at night. And a dorm full of brainwashed kids hanging on my every word. I wouldn't be able to live with myself."

"So, then, I disappoint you, too?" Lucien asked, appearing amused.

"*Disgust* is more the word I'd use."

Lucien nodded, as if to accept it. He held up an inquiring finger. "Let me ask you this,

Caylin, or whatever your name may be. Do you see anything in that temple to suggest that my students are unhappy? Brainwashed? Being held against their will?"

Caylin didn't answer.

"I'll take your silence as a no," Lucien said. "You see, they're devoted. But not devoted the way you might be devoted to whatever agency sent you here. They are . . . saturated. There isn't any part of them that isn't completely dedicated to what we're teaching here. Most of them have forgotten that another world exists outside these walls. They have found true peace. A true utopia. A true home."

"A place to stash their parents' cash," Caylin corrected, fists balled tightly.

Lucien rolled his eyes. "If you found your version of paradise, wouldn't you offer every penny you had to keep it?"

"Every penny converted into unmarked hundred-dollar bills," Caylin countered, her expression defiant. "Shipped out in small deposits to banks in the city. Marked down as donations. Then run through a complex computerized accounting system that makes every transaction untraceable. A system guarded by government-level watchdog security. Probably pirated from the CIA off the black market." She folded her arms and smirked. "Stop me if I'm wrong."

"I couldn't stop you if you were," Lucien replied dryly. A smile curled his lips. "You were definitely one of my gabbier students."

"Shame you didn't teach me anything," she said, gesturing to the roomful of cash. "I had to do an independent study to get what I was looking for."

"Okay, Caylin," Lucien said darkly, stepping forward menacingly. "The insult game is over. Who are you working for?"

At last, Caylin thought. The ruthless criminal comes out.

She took an instinctive step back but held up a brave front, saying nothing.

Lucien's expression intensified. His sparkling blue eyes nearly simmered in their sockets. "I ask again, who are you working for?"

Caylin glared at him, but kept silent.

"Well, it seems that this conversation is now over." He smirked, stroking his chin. "Such a pity. You brought me such nice, crisp hundred-dollar bills."

"Can we kill her?" one of the shaved heads asked.

A chill ran up Caylin's spine.

Lucien thought about it. A smile curled his lips. "No," he said. "Bring the car around. Let's take her to work."

J o slammed into the back of Theresa, and the
two of them belly flopped down the rusty
stairs. Theresa's hand shot out and snagged the
steel railing, bringing both of them to a tense, pan-
icky halt.

Whoa, she thought. That was close. Another
inch and she would've rolled right to the bottom of the steps.

"You okay?" Jo whispered from behind her.

"You mean other than my arm being torn
from its socket?" Theresa asked angrily. "I see
those ballet lessons are finally paying off."

"Sorry, T.," Jo said. "I slipped."

"I noticed."

Theresa continued forward shakily, trying to
flex the pain from her limbs. She was going to
have bruises on bruises after this mission. She
reached the bottom of the steps without tripping
over her own feet, then ducked to the side behind a large canvas cart full of cloth. Jo was next
to her in seconds.

"See?" Theresa said breathlessly, her heart hammering. "Piece of cake."

"Yeah, but you're about as graceful as a cow. Keep going—I want to get out of here." Jo pointed to the next cart. "That way."

They shuffled to the next cart almost on their hands and knees. They paused when a huge guard sauntered by, puffing on a nasty-looking cigar. His teeth were brown, and he wore no shirt. Streams of oily sweat ran down his torso, and he had hair up his back to his shoulders.

He paused momentarily not five feet in front of them. But he was intent on several workers down the aisle who weren't hustling as fast as he liked.

Then the smell hit Theresa. Pure body odor. So intense that it felt like a dirty hand clamped over her nose.

Jo gripped Theresa's arm. "I think I'm gonna puke," she whispered.

"Steady," Theresa said, holding her nose.

The guard moved on down the aisle, barking in some unknown language. The smell lingered like a deep footprint.

Theresa glanced at Jo. Her hand was clamped over her mouth and nose, and her eyes were watering.

"It's *on* me, T.," Jo moaned. "The smell is on me—I can feel it!"

"Come on," Theresa urged. "Let's go find a nice sewer somewhere."

They peeked around the cart. The nearest guard was a dozen paces away. No better chance. They crawled to the next cart and paused. The guard had moved farther away.

Theresa was about to bolt for the doorway when she caught the eye of one of the workers. She froze, and Jo slammed into her. But Theresa couldn't move.

The slave was a middle-aged woman, but she looked much older. A young boy—probably her son—sat next to her. They worked the fabric through the machines together because they were obviously too exhausted to do it separately. The woman seemed to look right through Theresa, her face blank. Then she turned back to her work without a word.

Theresa gulped.

This was insane. She scanned some of the other workers. Men who looked like they were starving. Women who looked ancient. Children who looked ready to pass out at their machines.

"Look," Jo whispered, pointing.

There was a young woman not far away, maybe nineteen or twenty. But she looked more like forty.

"Is she American?" Jo asked.

Theresa shrugged. It was possible. But who could tell for sure with all the dirt and sweat?

Theresa forced herself to move on, her jaw set grimly.

Soon it was in sight. The only thing that stood between them and the archway was another cart, a pile of discarded cloth, and ten feet of open floor.

"Ready?" Theresa asked.

"Of course not," Jo replied.

Theresa smirked and got in position. The only guard near them had moved off. Several carts now blocked his line of sight.

"Now's our chance—go!" Jo urged.

Theresa bolted to the last cart. She slid along its far side and started climbing the pile of discarded cloth.

Someone groaned. A puff of smoke rose from the other side of the pile.

She froze.

What was that? Theresa inched farther up the pile, trying to see—

A guard sat up on the other side of the pile! Bits of cloth clung to his back like leeches. He groaned again, brushed some away, and stretched.

Theresa's eyes bugged, and panic shot through her like a thunderbolt.

He'd been dozing on the cloth pile! His stinky cigar was less than two feet from Theresa's face!

Theresa slid back down the pile and went into a fetal position. She frantically started burying herself in the pile of scrap. In seconds she was partially concealed—as long as she stayed still. She glared back at Jo. She had taken refuge behind the last cart. She was totally pale.

The guy looked around, still sleepy. He held his cigar, yawned, and smacked his lips.

He didn't see me, Theresa thought. He would've flipped by now.

But how were they going to get by him?

A voice barked from across the room. The guard scowled and looked that way. The voice came again. The guy grunted something back and waved. Then he stood and stretched. He shook his head like a dog and belched.

From the foul look on Jo's face, she was thinking the same thing as Theresa: What a pig!

The guard turned around then and marched right up and over the pile of scrap. On his way down the other side one big boot came down next to Theresa's nose. The other came down on her left hand.

It took all of her willpower not to scream.

The guy moved on, but Theresa pulled her hand back and held it. It throbbed hotly but seemed to be okay. Rage blossomed within her, and she wanted to pop that guy right in the kisser. After a flea bath, of course.

Then Theresa froze again.

The guard had paused next to the cart Jo was

hiding behind. She could've reached out and tugged on his greasy pants.

Jo glared at Theresa as if to ask, What now?

Theresa mouthed "don't move" and flexed her hurt hand. All either of them could do was stay still.

The guard fished in his pocket and pulled out a lighter. He flicked it, but nothing happened. Flicked it again. And again.

Theresa rolled her eyes. Come *on*.

Finally the lighter blazed to life. He put the flame to his dying cigar to freshen it. Puffs of smoke came up. Then he snapped the lighter shut, pocketed it, and admired his smoke. A dreamy look came over his face, and he puffed on it some more.

Then fresh panic rose in Theresa. From her angle she could see another guard—the big hairy head guard—approaching. He looked ticked. The other guard was too busy enjoying his cigar to see him.

He marched right up and smacked the stogie out of the guy's mouth! Red ashes and smoke shot up from the guy's face in a blizzard . . . and the cigar flipped over the cart and came down right on Jo's head!

Jo spazzed and knocked the chewed-up stump away, not stopping until all the burning ashes were out of her hair. Theresa had never seen such a look of pure rage on Jo's face. Her hair—in a tight ponytail before—was now everywhere. Her nostrils were flared nearly as wide as her eyes, and her breaths came in deep, heaving gulps.

The head guard bellowed a litany of insults. The smaller guard could only sit there and take it. But Theresa could see his eyes. . . . He was searching the floor for his cigar. And it was smoldering a few inches from Jo's right hand.

If he found the cigar, she was snagged for sure!

Theresa frantically tried to signal Jo, but she wasn't looking. She was too busy brushing the residual ashes from her hair.

"Come on, Jo, look!"

Finally Jo glanced her way. Theresa caught her eye and made sure she was paying attention. She held up her own right hand and pointed to it. Then she pointed at Jo's hand.

Jo looked down. And her eyes went wide.

The head guard finished screaming and walked away from the smaller guard. Immediately the smaller guard started searching for his lost cigar.

At that instant Jo flicked it with her finger. It spun out from behind the cart and came to a stop right by the guy's foot.

He smiled, picked it up, and put it back in his mouth. The guard walked away, happily flicking his dead lighter.

Theresa let out a huge sigh and crawled out

from under the cloth. Jo shuffled forward and met her behind the last cart. She immediately parted her hair for Theresa and bared her skull.

"Do I have a burn?" she demanded. "I swear it feels like I have a burn."

"I don't see anything, Jo," Theresa replied wearily. "Let's go."

"Ooo, I wanted to hit that guy! What a walking trash bag!"

"Come on," Theresa pleaded, tugging Jo's arm.

She took one last look around. The coast was as clean as could be, all guards' hygiene considered.

They bolted across the last ten feet and through the archway. Once outside the shop they stopped for a breath.

"I don't think anyone saw us," Theresa said.

"Except that woman and her son," Jo replied, her face full of disgust. "I mean . . . T., we have to *do* something—"

"I know, Jo. I know. But we can't do anything until we get out of here and contact Uncle Sam. Okay?"

Jo nodded. "Yeah. Let's go."

The corridors were damp and fetid. Being so close to the harbor brought in the moisture. The rats had to be huge. Luckily they didn't see any— it was too dark. Unfortunately that meant that they couldn't see any guards up ahead. They would literally run right into them. And that would be the end of them.

But Theresa and Jo knew they didn't have a choice. If they didn't make it out of this maze, then no one would ever know what was going on underneath that warehouse. It would open up as that recreation center, and pampered children of all ages would be playing games up there while people of all ages rotted away down here.

They *had* to make it out. It was that simple.

Soon Theresa felt a breeze from up ahead.

"Is that a way out?" Jo asked, peering through the gloom.

"I don't see any lights," Theresa whispered. "And that air isn't exactly fresh. I wouldn't get your hopes up."

With that, they stepped into a wide chamber. A few propane torches hung along the walls, but not much to see by. Yet Theresa saw all she needed to see.

They were in a cell block. Prison bars ran along both walls, and behind them hundreds of workers slept. But the conditions were hardly humane. They slept in tight groups on cloth mats woven from scraps. Bowls and jars lined the floors of the cells, but Theresa couldn't tell if the workers ate out of them, drank out of them, or . . .

"Oh no," Jo moaned. "Oh, Theresa . . ."

Theresa squeezed Jo's hand. "Shhh, I know. Let's keep moving."

They moved down the corridor between the cells, careful not to make a sound. It would've been bad enough to wake up the workers, who would no doubt beg to be set free. But it would've been worse to wake up the two snoring guards at the far end of the chamber. They were stretched out in their chairs, feet and arms crossed, heads back and mouths open. Sawing away.

"When we get out of here, T., I'm going to make it my mission in life to see that Lucien West never sees another ray of sunlight for the rest of his life. I'm going to bury him," Jo seethed.

"We all are, Jo. I promise you. But we have to get out of here first."

They edged closer to the snoring guards. Jo tiptoed up to them and delicately stepped over them. Then she turned back to Theresa and motioned for her to do the same.

Theresa did. But in midstep one of the guards stopped snoring.

She froze, one foot dangling in the air.

The guard grunted, shifted, smacked his lips, and continued snoring.

Carefully Theresa licked her lips and stepped over him.

They moved on into the darkness. The tunnels seemed endless. The warehouse took up an entire block, but this maze went on and on. They had to be beyond the borders of the warehouse. Who knew where they would come out?

Finally Theresa saw a light up ahead.

"I hope that's a door," Jo said. "And there's a spa on the other side of it. A spa with Swedish masseurs and hot mud and a mineral water Jacuzzi."

"I'll settle for the door," Theresa replied.

But it wasn't a door. It was another chamber. It was better lit than the others, with half a dozen electric bulbs hanging from the ceiling. There were three tables in the room, with two bulbs above each one.

But that's not what stopped the Spy Girls dead.

It was the three army-green suitcases, one on each table. The ones with the Russian writing on the side. Poised nice and neat. As if in respect. Or on display.

No guards were there to greet them. Just the girls and the suitcases.

"Those are the cases from the truck," Jo whispered.

"I knew there had to be gold at the end of this nightmare rainbow," Theresa replied.

They opened one and flipped back the lid. Then another. And another.

And froze.

Theresa's heart felt like it was in her throat,

and Jo stood there with her mouth hanging open.

No one said a word. No one had to.

Theresa knew from her training what she was looking at. It seemed impossible. But it wasn't. The proof was right there in front of her.

The cases held the components of a nuclear warhead, ready for assembly!

Oh no," Theresa muttered, gripping a table for support.

"Is that what I think it is?" Jo asked wearily, pointing at a section of the device and hoping, hoping that it wasn't . . .

But she knew it was.

"It sure isn't lost luggage from Siberia," Theresa replied.

Jo thought about that. "Actually, it *is*."

"The real question is, what do we do about it?" Theresa asked, delicately fingering a piece of hardware.

"Do you remember when Uncle Sam briefed us on Carruthers?" Jo asked, allowing herself to touch the device as well, knowing in the pit of her stomach what it was capable of. "He said the guy was affiliated with a terrorist group trying to smuggle nuclear weapons out of Russia."

"Looks like he succeeded," Theresa commented, gesturing to the cases.

"Indeed, he did," came a voice from behind them. They whirled.

An extremely handsome man stood before them. He had black hair that came to a pronounced widow's peak. His eyes were deep-set, but incredibly bright and piercing. He was dressed in a pair of slacks and a pullover shirt. Very neat, yet not what they expected from a renowned religious leader.

He was surrounded by half a dozen armed guards, all with shaved heads.

And next to him stood a familiar form, dressed in white sweats and slippers.

Caylin!

"Mr. Carruthers, I presume," Jo said with a smile.

Lucien chuckled. "I'm sorry, dear. You must have me mixed up with someone else. My name is West. Lucien West."

"You don't look so 'luscious' to me," Theresa muttered.

"He's not," Caylin agreed.

At that comment Lucien shoved Caylin forward. She stumbled over to her comrades. "Why don't you stand with your friends, Caylin. I've had quite enough of you."

"Yeah, you're a real one-man party yourself, Carruthers," Caylin replied. She smiled at Jo and Theresa. "How are you guys doing?"

"We were fine until *you* got here," Theresa replied.

"When did you get busted, Cay?" Jo asked.

"About an hour ago," Caylin replied.

"Sloppy," Jo chided. "That's a whole hour before us. We win." She grinned triumphantly.

"Maybe so," Caylin responded. "But I picked a lock with a bobby pin in less than a minute. And that's in the field!"

"You're lying," Theresa muttered, shaking her head. "No way. Not in under a minute."

"I sure did!" Caylin protested.

"Not a chance," Jo agreed.

"Just ask Lucien, girls. His security cameras have it on tape." Caylin glared at Lucien. "Tell them, Lucien. And while you're at it, tell them about the rec room in your basement that's filled to the ceiling with hundred-dollar bills."

"Cool," Theresa said.

"That's my kind of rec room," Jo added.

"If you girls are quite finished, we have some business to attend to," Lucien said with a smile. "So if you'll just tell me who you're working for, we can get on to the unpleasant part of the evening."

"Working for?" Theresa asked, raising her eyebrows.

"We don't think of this as work," Jo said, buffing her nails. "It's more of a spiritual thing."

"Yeah," Caylin agreed, clapping a hand on

Theresa's shoulder. "We go around the world exposing trash bag con men for the vermin that they are. Then—*bam*—instant inner peace. You understand, don't you?"

Lucien shut his eyes and rubbed his head like it hurt. "No, I don't think I do," he muttered.

Theresa stepped forward. "Why don't I give it a try?" she asked. "It goes something like this. The cult is a front for the sweatshop. You launder all the cash that comes in from knockoff clothing by running it through the cult's books. You make all the money look like cash donations. Nice and legal."

"But the one question that's been nagging us," Jo went on, arms held out expansively, "is, why all the cash? I mean, you have way more cash than you could ever generate from knockoffs. So where did it all come from?" Her eyes narrowed, and she pointed at the nuke. "Our answer's right there on those tables, isn't it?"

Caylin nodded. "You've been using your terrorist contacts to get the nukes. Then you're selling them to the highest bidder."

"That's what you're calling 'the Purchase' in all your ledgers," Theresa said. She folded her arms across her chest and smiled. "By the way. Your computer security systems stink. I broke right in and downloaded the whole thing. You really should have your security beefed up. Any old moron can hack in there. Very sloppy."

"So," Jo asked, shrugging. "Does that just about cover it?"

Lucien broke out into gales of laughter. The girls didn't even crack a smile. "No," he said, snickering. "You're wrong. You're completely wrong."

Theresa's brow furrowed. "I doubt it," she replied. "We're pretty good at this stuff. And you're not that smart."

Lucien beamed. "Oh yes, I am."

"Prove it," Jo challenged.

"As I told Caylin, the temple is quite legitimate," Lucien replied. He paced the floor as he spoke, slipping into preacher mode. "All the students are there because they want to be. I don't brainwash. I just happen to have something that they crave."

"It can't be charm," Jo said with a disgusted scowl.

"No, Jo," Caylin said as she leaned closer to her friend. "The word's *smarm*."

Lucien shook his head. "Try empathy, ladies. Empathy. I feel their pain. I accept them for who they are. I let them become who they've always wanted to be. It's really very simple." Lucien ran a hand along the lid of one of the green cases and gently shut it. Then he smiled. "As for the money-laundering part, yes, that's true. But that's just on the surface. It's how I got started in Kinh-Sanh five years ago."

"Is he always this wordy?" Theresa asked Caylin.

"Oh yeah," Caylin answered immediately.

"Great. Should we sit down?" Jo asked sarcastically.

"No," Lucien ordered, pointing a menacing finger at them. "Stand. For it's really quite fascinating."

"It is?" Jo griped.

"Shhh, Jo," Theresa whispered. "The guy's giving it all up."

Lucien moved to the remaining cases as he spoke, shutting and latching them in turn. "The shop and the temple ran smoothly for a few years. But then the Kinh-Sanh government tried to shut down the shop as a goodwill gesture to the United States. You know, a little brown nosing by the third world country to impress the Yanks. I was desperate. I would've been out of business. And this was the best operation I had ever set up. It was perfect."

"So you *are* Carruthers," Caylin pointed out.

"If you say so, Caylin," he replied, shrugging. "It hardly matters. Anyway, I had to find a way to keep the dream alive. So I went to the prime minister of Kinh-Sanh and made him an offer he couldn't refuse."

"And that was?" Theresa asked.

Lucien's grin was sinister. "I would help him make Kinh-Sanh a major world power overnight. A country that would be more powerful than all of its neighbors. A country that could stand proudly and point to its beautiful capital city, its clean streets, and its friendly natives, and say, 'Kinh-Sanh's voice will now be heard around the world.'"

The realization hit Jo like a thunderbolt. It must have hit the other girls as well because Theresa blurted out: "You're selling the prime minister the nukes!"

"Selling?" Lucien asked impatiently.

Jo chuckled. "Oh, sorry, I guess you're just *giving* them to him," she mused.

"That's exactly what I'm doing," Lucien replied, patting one of the cases. "Make no mistake, he's paying for them. But I'm acting as a broker, so to speak."

Great, Jo thought. Just what the world needs. A trash bag of nuclear proportions.

"The almighty middleman," Caylin muttered.

"Precisely," Lucien said. "I get a hefty 'finder's fee' and the eternal gratitude of the prime minister. He immediately saw the light when it came to my other operations. The shop keeps his streets free of unsightly homeless people, which brings in the tourists, which brings in the cash. In exchange, I get a cut of the pie."

"So that's it?" Theresa asked.

"Not quite," Lucien replied smugly. "I also get to operate my businesses unchallenged. You see, believe it or not, I *am* a spiritual man. But I am also a big believer in free enterprise. And this nuclear-sized deal will not just tip the scales of world order, it'll make me a billionaire in the process."

"At the cost of hundreds of lives in your shop," Theresa said in disgust.

"Or millions if those nukes ever get used," Caylin added grimly.

Lucien only smiled and spread his arms. "Name a billionaire who hasn't squashed a few hundred lives in his day?"

Jo started laughing. Laughing hard. She felt the other girls staring at her, probably wondering if she'd snapped.

"Something amusing?" Lucien asked, glaring at her.

Jo giggled, nodding. "Yeah, big time. You've formulated the perfect plan here, Carruthers. But it's not quite perfect."

Lucien smiled pleasantly. "No?"

"No. You left out one tiny but crucial detail."

Lucien's smile became a smirk. "Well? Are you going to enlighten me?"

"Showers, Lucien. Showers for your guards! They stink! They stink worse than my high school football team, and they practiced in a cow pasture!"

Lucien couldn't suppress his own chuckle. He turned to his guards. "Well, gentlemen, what do you think about that?"

The biggest, hairiest guard stepped forward.

He smiled at Jo. Jo smiled back nervously. Then her nervousness turned to horror as she watched the man lift his arm and literally blow his body odor toward them!

"How disgusting!" Jo moaned, fanning with her hand. "Why don't you just cut me in half with a laser or something quick?"

The guards chuckled and slapped their smelly comrade on the back for his ingenuity.

"What a shame that all this is for nothing," Theresa said to Lucien. "Our people will be along any minute now. And then it's bye-bye, Carruthers."

Lucien laughed even harder. "So what? Let them come. What do you think they'll find? An empty warehouse. Meanwhile you three will be earning back all the money you've cost me by standing here talking."

"What do you mean?" Caylin asked uneasily.

Lucien nodded to his guards. "Put these young ladies to work. Give them their own machines. And let them sew until they either die of exhaustion or dehydration." The smile widened on his face. "Whichever comes first."

Caylin squinted at her dark, murky surroundings as the Spy Girls were led back to the sweatshop. All the tired, tortured eyes of the workers focused on her and her friends as they were searched. The guards took all their gear. Everything. Then they sat the girls down in a row in front of three decrepit sewing machines and shackled their ankles to a steel bar underneath.

Caylin tested the bonds. Solid. Very solid. And heavy. Caylin knew she was in shape—but she wondered how the slaves could even move their feet on the sewing machine pedals. They looked so skinny and weak.

We'll look like that, too, if we don't do something, she thought.

Huge piles of unsewn sleeves were slapped down before them. The big hairy guard ran down the instructions, plain and simple. The Spy Girls were to sew the long hem the length of the sleeve, making a tube. Someone else would be sewing them to the body.

The guard lit a new cigar and spit on the floor. "Here are rules," he barked in a thick accent. "Work or else. That's it. Simple, no?"

"No," Jo replied. "We don't know how to sew."

The guard, obviously knowing how much he turned Jo on, leaned in real close and puffed his cigar. Jo looked as if she wanted to puke then and there. "Is even more simple. Learn or else."

The guard blew a massive cloud of smoke in Jo's face. He walked away, laughing.

"I'll never wash this stink off me," Jo moaned. "It'll be on me forever, I know it."

"If we don't get out of here," Theresa warned, "forever will be sooner than you think."

The guard snapped his fingers at them.

"Guess we better start sewing," Caylin suggested, picking up a sleeve. "How do we do this?"

"T., your mom's a designer," Jo said. "Did she ever teach you anything about sewing?"

Theresa shrugged, awkwardly holding a piece of fabric. "As far as I know, all you do is take the sleeve, fold it over like this, and run it straight through the machine like this."

She pressed the pedal and ran it through the machine. The needle chomped into the fabric and ate it up in seconds. Theresa held up her work so they could see.

"Nice work, T.," Jo replied. "Olive Oyl couldn't even get her hand through that cuff."

She was right, Caylin saw. Theresa had sewn a crooked line to the end, leaving a one-inch hole where someone's hand was supposed to come through.

"Oh, well," Theresa said, shrugging. "That's the theory."

They all started sewing their sleeves. Badly. Very, very badly. But Caylin didn't care. Jo reasoned that the more sleeves they ruined, the less business Lucien would have. So they kept sewing and didn't make any attempt to improve. But after a few minutes something was strange.

"Do you suddenly feel like a celebrity?" Jo asked.

"I know what you mean," Caylin replied, creeped out.

All around them the workers stared. It must have been a big event—three American girls being brought in at gunpoint and chained. But after a while, and a little prodding from the guards, everyone settled back into their routine of ordinary, everyday slave labor. And the guards resumed their lounging and joking among themselves.

That's when the Spy Girls came to life.

"It's time for a plan," Caylin said out of the side of her mouth.

"Any suggestions?" Jo asked, glancing at the guards.

"They took everything," Theresa replied.

The girls spoke in low voices, not looking at each other. Caylin and the others tried to make it seem as if they were working, working, working, just like everyone else.

"Not everything," Jo said with a sly grin.

"Really?" Theresa asked. "What do you have left?"

"My heel."

Realization dawned on Caylin. Of course! Theresa and Jo still wore their Tower-issue shoes. Each pair was equipped with one homing beacon in the left heel. All you had to do was slide it out—which they both did nonchalantly—touch it with your thumbprint, and slide it back into place. Supposedly a distress signal was now being sent to the nearest Tower receiver. But who knew where that was? Or if the signal could get out of the subbasement at all?

"Let's hope the cavalry is on its way," Caylin said, sloppily running a sleeve through her machine.

"We can't count on it," Theresa said gravely. "I have another idea."

Caylin watched as Theresa motioned to the nearest guard. He scowled and reluctantly came over.

"Hello, sir," Theresa said sweetly. "I hate to bother you, but you guys confiscated my glasses. I can't see a thing without them. Look at this terrible job I'm doing." She held up some of the useless sleeves she'd sewn. "Silly me. I'm blind as a bat!"

The guard shrugged. He didn't speak English. And he obviously didn't care.

Jo grinned as soon as she heard the word *glasses*.

Caylin scowled. What's going on? she wondered. What's with the glasses?

Theresa raised her voice. "Do you understand me? I need my glasses! I can't see anything without them! Blind. Do you understand the word *blind*? It means I can't see what I'm doing. I could be setting world underground sewing records if I could just see what I was doing! Where's your boss? Bring him over." Theresa stood and waved to the big hairy guard with the cigar. "Yoo-hoo! Hairy guard! You speak English. Can you get my glasses for me? Please?"

The cigar-chomping guard shambled over, a look of supreme rage on his face. "What you want?"

"My glasses." Theresa traced circles around her eyes and pointed at the pile of Spy Girl gear over by the stairs. "I need them to see. See?" She squinted for emphasis.

"You get glasses. You shut up and work."

Theresa nodded vigorously. "Oh yes, absolutely. I promise."

The guard chewed on his cigar for a moment, thinking. Then he marched over to the pile of gear. He held up Jo's fanny pack.

"No, that's not it," Theresa said. "It's the one

underneath. Yeah, that's the one. My glasses are in there. Thanks so much."

The guard brought Theresa her glasses. She gratefully put them on and picked up a sleeve. "Oh, what a beautiful pattern. I hadn't noticed it before."

"You work now," the guard growled, threatening to backhand her. "Or else."

Theresa humbly bowed and smiled. "Oh yes, I promise. You're a very nice man. I take away all the things she said about you." Theresa pointed to Jo. "She didn't mean it, really."

When the guard was out of earshot, T. added, "Except the part about you *stinking*."

"What's the big deal about your glasses?" Caylin demanded.

Theresa turned to Caylin and smiled. "Watch your feet, Spy Girl. The heat's on."

With that, she began to laser through Caylin's shackles.

"Yow!" Caylin barked as the red beams cut into the steel around her ankles. "What's *that?*"

"That's hot," Theresa warned, her eyes focused intensely. "So don't move."

Caylin grimaced, waiting for the laser to cut into her flesh. But it never did. The whole process took only a few seconds. Suddenly the shackles clanked open at her feet.

Theresa quickly did the same for Jo's and her own.

They were free . . . sort of.

"What do we do about the guards?" Jo whispered. "We can't just sneak out."

Caylin smiled. "Hey, T."

Theresa looked at her. Caylin subtly pointed at the ceiling. Theresa saw what she meant and grinned.

"Hold on to your butts," Theresa warned.

She fixed her laser gaze skyward and activated it. A red beam shot up to the ceiling. Caylin's smile widened as Theresa hit her target.

"What's she doing?" Jo whispered.

"Watch," Caylin answered.

It became quite clear when the sprinkler head Theresa hit got hot enough to go off.

Within seconds the whole sprinkler system went off, drenching the whole shop.

A fire alarm sounded, and the guards scrambled around in confusion.

Caylin grinned in the downpour.

"Let's get out of here!" she cried.

aylin looked around at the sheer madness breaking out around her. The guards were too busy trying to figure out where the fire was—and how to shut off the sprinklers—to care that the Spy Girls sprinted across the shop to the archway. The girls ran through, leaving the screaming workers pulling at their shackles as the place was soaked.

But the storm didn't stop at the exit. The sprinkler system ran throughout the tunnels, and the Spy Girls raced through them, covering their eyes and trying not to slip on the slimy stone floor.

"Do you guys know where you're going?" Caylin yelled, hoping against hope.

"Trust us," Jo called back. "We've done this before."

Two soaked guards met them head-on, but they didn't stop them. The confused men ran right past them.

"Did they even see us?" Theresa asked.

"Who cares?" Jo cried. "Go!"

167

Soon they reached the prison block. The water and screaming alarm had awakened the workers. They waved their arms and cried out to be freed. Some slammed cups and debris against the bars, trying to get their attention.

"Oh no," Jo wailed. "The workers! We have to help them!"

"How do we let them out?" Theresa asked, looking around helplessly.

"Over there," Caylin said, pointing to a series of levers on the far wall.

"Are you sure?" Theresa called.

"Of course not!" Caylin sprinted over and began yanking every lever on down the line. Sure enough, one by one the cell doors clanked open!

"You did it!" Jo screamed as scores of slaves poured out of their cells.

They all jumped around and celebrated in the sprinkler-induced rainfall, letting it douse them in newfound freedom. They howled their thanks to the Spy Girls in words they couldn't understand. But the message was obvious.

Just then a pair of guards entered.

The slaves took one look at their captors and charged them. The guards' eyes bulged, and they scrambled to escape. But there was nowhere to go. Twenty slaves landed on top of them.

The men screamed, but they were overmatched. Soon they were just the bottom of a huge human pile. A twisted mass of limbs and fists.

Finally a skinny Kinh-Sanh man stood up, holding his fist high. In it he held a ring of shackle keys.

He screamed something and pointed back toward the sweatshop. His brethren roared their approval. The sea of slaves headed in that direction, no doubt intending to free all their friends and relatives on the sewing machines.

As the riot moved away Caylin noticed the two guards. They staggered to their feet and moved in a panicked daze toward the shop, ignoring the Spy Girls.

"That should keep those guards busy for a while," Jo said, beaming.

"Keep them busy?" Caylin scoffed. "Those cowards will hightail it to the nearest horizon the first chance they get."

"Let's go get that nuke," Theresa said, pointing down the hall.

"And a certain trash bag, too," Caylin added, jaw set.

They sprinted down the tunnel. When they burst into the well-lit chamber, it was empty.

And so were the tables!

Caylin's heart sank. Her fists involuntarily balled at her sides, and she wanted to throw something. Hard.

"He's got the nuke," Jo said helplessly.

"You don't say," Caylin responded, rage in her voice.

Theresa pointed at a doorway in the far wall. "That's the only way out. He had to go that way."

"Let's roll!" Caylin cried, racing forward.

The tunnel grew very dark very quickly. The sprinkler system didn't reach that far, but the moisture was intense. The stone floor was as slick as ice in some places. And the smell of dead fish grew unbearable. Where were they going?

Soon Caylin heard lapping waves along with their labored breathing.

"The harbor must be close," Jo said, puffing.

Finally the trio emerged in a stone, cavelike chamber. The ceiling was low and wet. Before them was a dock. Two massive powerboats were moored there. The water came in from the mouth of the cave, which seemed to open into the harbor. The first light of dawn made the mouth seem like a glowing portal to another world.

In a way, it was.

"Hold it right there, ladies!" came an angry voice.

Lucien stood up in one of the powerboats. He leveled a submachine gun at them.

The Spy Girls came to a dead stop, nearly sliding right into the water on the slick stone.

A black tarp covered much of the seating area

of Lucien's powerboat. No doubt where he had stashed the nuclear suitcases.

"Give it up, Carruthers," Theresa warned, stepping forward. "It's all finished."

"Are you *kidding?*" Lucien asked incredulously. "I'm the one holding the gun. I'm the one holding the nuclear weapon and a ton of cash. I'm not finished. I'm just getting started."

"That's a Furious Shepherd," Jo whispered to Caylin.

"*What?*" Caylin asked.

"The boat," Jo replied. "Both of them. The Furious Shepherd 76. One of the fastest boats on the water." She smiled at Lucien. "I'm impressed, sleezeball."

"How sweet," Lucien replied, rolling his eyes. "Then you probably won't understand it when I do this."

He turned the machine gun on the other boat and opened fire. Bullets sprayed the control panel and driver's seat of the beautiful boat, shredding it. He also raked the gun across the boat's stern, riddling the fuel tank until the gun was empty. The boat was now useless.

"You are truly a criminal," Jo said, staring forlornly at the ruined machine.

Lucien yanked the empty clip from the gun. "I can't very well have you coming after me, can I? You know, in the big climactic boat chase? No,

I'm afraid not. I'm afraid I'll just have to set sail into a beautiful sunrise. The perfect beginning to a brand-new day."

"How can you live with what you have done?" Caylin asked.

Lucien shrugged. "It's just a boat."

Caylin scowled. "Not that. Your students. Your disciples. Your devoted followers who have invested everything they have—financially and spiritually—just to be a part of your world?"

Caylin stood defiantly, and Lucien paused. He seemed to think about it. Really think about it.

"It wasn't fake," he said softly, eyes distant. "They're good kids. They've learned a lot. I've helped them."

Caylin's lip curled into a snarl. "And now you're dumping them. Do you have any idea what's going to happen to them when they find out what you really are?"

Lucien's eyes regained their focus, once again zeroing in on Caylin. "They're young. They'll get over it."

"You disgusting piece of—," Caylin began.

"Oh, spare me, Caylin," Lucien snapped, grabbing a fresh clip for his gun. "People expect way too much from leaders. They need to think for themselves." He chuckled humorlessly. "No one was ever around to help *me*."

"It shows," Caylin replied stiffly.

Lucien smiled and hefted the clip. "Good-bye, beautiful Caylin."

Just as Lucien was about to shove the fresh clip into the gun, the doorway behind the Spy Girls exploded with slaves.

They poured through the opening, aiming all their pent-up rage at the man in the boat. The man responsible for their slavery. For the torture and the inhuman living conditions. For *everything*.

Lucien couldn't get the gun loaded fast enough. And even if he did, he never would have had enough bullets. They stormed the boat and beat him down, tearing the gun away and tossing it into the water. They ripped at his clothes and hair. Blood poured from his nose, and finally Luscious Lucien West screamed in true fear. He went into a fetal position and waited for the bitter end.

"We can't let them do it," Jo whispered. "As much as he deserves it. As much as *they* deserve it. We can't let it happen."

Caylin glanced at Theresa, who nodded. Unfortunately Jo was right.

The Spy Girls ran forward and began pulling the slaves from Lucien. They held them back and explained that he must go to jail. It was only right. They explained that if they killed Lucien, then they would be no better than Lucien. The Kinh-Sanh government couldn't and wouldn't protect him. The government was in as much trouble for conspiring with him.

"But what do we have if we let him live?" asked one freed slave in broken English.

"Your freedom," Theresa explained.

"That's lame," Caylin said. She reached under the tarp and pulled out one of Lucien's infamous cash cubes. All U.S. hundred-dollar bills. "How about your freedom . . . and a big hunk of money!"

The people cheered, and Caylin started handing out thick wads of bills. The people grabbed the money, pouncing and fondling it like a belated Christmas gift. Ben Franklins fluttered everywhere, and the joyous workers scrambled for the dropped cash as if they were on a game show.

"Well, I feel a lot better," Jo said. She nudged Lucien with her elbow. "How about you?"

"Leave me alone," Lucien mumbled, trying to hold back the blood from his nose.

"Hey, Jo," Caylin said. "You say this is one of the fastest boats on the water?"

"You know it," Jo said.

Caylin smiled. "Well, then fire the puppy up!"

"No!" Theresa piped up. "No way! She is not driving this thing. I almost got squashed by a truck because of her driving. *I'll* drive."

"*You?*" Jo asked. "You couldn't find the ignition switch in this rig. And it was your fat rear end that kept me from being able to swing around that truck!"

"Yo, Spy Girls, chill your engines," Caylin said. "Let's just get out of this cave. I'm getting claustrophobic."

Jo fired up the twin engines and slowly guided the Furious Shepherd into the harbor. The sun was just rising over the eastern horizon, bathing them in a warm orange light.

That's when Jo floored it.

"That's far enough," Caylin said.

Jo cut the engines. The bow of the monster boat slowly returned to the surface of the water. They had run out to the middle of the harbor, about a mile from shore.

Jo shut down the engines completely. All they heard was the lapping of the waves and the cries of seabirds.

After a few minutes Lucien looked up at them. "Are you going to kill me?"

Jo laughed.

"Nope," Caylin said. "Not to say that you don't deserve it."

"Then what are we waiting for?" he asked, mopping blood from his upper lip.

Suddenly a huge disturbance in the water made the boat rock.

"*That's* what we're waiting for," Theresa said.

She grabbed the nearest railing. "Better hold on tight, Luscious."

The sea churned all around them, bubbling and roaring as if Godzilla himself was coming up.

But it wasn't Godzilla. In seconds they saw a huge black shape rise up not far off their starboard side. Then something slammed the boat from underneath. Something *huge*.

It lifted the boat clear out of the water. The craft pitched to one side and came to rest on the deck of a long, black sea monster. A steel sea monster known as the U.S.S. *Manhattan,* a nuclear submarine.

Soon the waves settled as the sub surfaced completely. All was calm around them. Then they heard a familiar voice come over the sub's loudspeaker.

"Welcome aboard, Spy Girls," Uncle Sam declared. "Mission accomplished!"

EPILOGUE

I can't believe you're actually wearing that," Theresa scolded Jo as she paraded shamelessly around the Kinh-Sanh flat. It was their last day in the country, after a long and boring debriefing.

"Why not?" Jo asked, modeling one of the obnoxious designer knockoffs she'd bought at the street market. "It's fabu."

"I knew it!" Theresa exclaimed. "You are such a liar. You said it was a clue, and that was it. You said you wouldn't be caught wearing it at your own funeral, remember?"

"Shut up, T.," Jo warned, holding up a finger.

"In fact," Theresa continued, marching forward, "you said you wouldn't be caught dead wearing it—"

"Theresa, shut up!" Jo said.

"*At Mike Schaeffer's funeral!*" Theresa finished, getting in Jo's face.

"Who's Mike Schaeffer?" Caylin asked, guzzling a soda.

"An old flame, apparently," Theresa teased. "I couldn't get it out of her."

"Jo, how interesting," Caylin said, playing with her straw. "Tell me more."

"Since when do you care about my love life?" Jo grumbled.

Caylin shrugged and smiled. "Since it makes you so uncomfortable."

The Spy Girls were understandably punchy. The week following Lucien's capture had been one long meeting after another. The scam they had uncovered reached all the way to the prime minister of Kinh-Sanh himself. Upon the country's learning of the scandal, he was immediately arrested. The capital city exploded in celebration at the news. It was like one long Mardi Gras that the Spy Girls couldn't enjoy because they were telling so many bureaucrats exactly what had happened. Ugh, how utterly boring.

"Do you know that I've shampooed twice a day for a week, and I still smell cigar smoke in my hair?" Jo grumbled, holding a few strands in front of her face for inspection. "It's amazing. I told you it would happen. I'm going to have to carry this around with me like luggage. No guy will ever want to come near me."

"Enough about the cigar smoke!" Caylin bellowed, holding up her hands. "I've had it up to here with the cigar smoke!"

Jo grabbed up her own soda and sipped it. "If you have something better to talk about, Cay, let's hear it."

"How about Mike Schaeffer?" Theresa asked, arching an eyebrow.

"*Except* Mike Schaeffer," Jo warned.

"How about our next mission?" Caylin suggested, kicking aside one of the throw pillows. "All the stupid meetings are over. World peace reigns once again. What's our next move?"

"Sammy hasn't said anything," Theresa replied. "Maybe we're just heading back home for now."

"Good. I could use the sleep," Jo muttered, massaging her temples.

"Not so fast, Spy Girls," came Sammy's familiar voice.

Caylin jumped up from the sea of pillows. "I *hate* when you do that, Uncle Sam," she bristled, shaking her fist at the ceiling. "How long have you been listening to us?"

"Long enough to know I don't want to know a thing about Mike Schaeffer."

"You're the only one," Jo commented.

"So what's the deal, Sammy?" Theresa asked, glancing around the room. "Where are we off to this time?"

Sammy chuckled. "Well, Spy Girls, you handled yourselves so well on this mission, we've come up with something even more interesting."

"Is world peace in danger?" Theresa asked hopefully.

"Definitely," Sam answered.

"Is it in an exotic foreign land?" Caylin asked.

"Absolutely."

Jo mugged at her partners mischievously. "Will there be cute guys to stare at?"

Theresa and Caylin moaned and threw pillows at her.

"Can't you keep your mind out of the gutter for ten seconds?" Caylin asked.

"Oh, like you weren't thinking it," Jo replied, shoving pillows away. "I mean, really. Sometimes I think I'm the only one who tells it like it is around here."

"Excuse me, girls," Sam interrupted. "Should I come back later?"

"Of course not," Theresa replied. "If Jo would shut up long enough for you to talk."

Jo tossed a pillow back at Theresa but didn't reply.

"Very well," Sam continued. "You would like to know the location of your next mission?"

"Yes," they said simultaneously.

Uncle Sam chuckled. "Okay, Spy Girls. Your wish is my command. Hang on to your socks because you're off to . . ."

About the Author

Elizabeth Cage is a saucy pseudonym for a noted young adult writer. Her true identity and current whereabouts are classified.

ROSWELL HIGH

He's not like other guys.

Liz has seen him around. It's hard to miss Max—the tall, blond, blue-eyed senior stands out in her high-school crowd. So why is he such a loner?

Max is in love with Liz. He loves the way her eyes light up when she laughs. And the way her long, black hair moves when she turns her head. Most of all, he loves to imagine what it would be like to kiss her.

But Max knows he can't get too close. He can't let her discover the truth about who he is. Or really, what he is....Because the truth could kill her.

One astounding secret...a shared moment of danger...life will never be the same.

A new series by Melinda Metz

Available from Archway Paperbacks
Published by Pocket Books

2034